Monica Dickens, great-granddaughter of Charles Dickens, has written over forty novels, autobiographical books and children's books. Her first book, *One Pair of Hands*, which arose out of her experiences as a cook and general servant, made her a best-seller at twenty-two, and is still in great demand. Her books reflect the varied aspects of a full and eventful life. Three years' wartime nursing led to *One Pair of Feet* and *The Happy Prisoner*. After a year in an aircraft factory she wrote *The Fancy*, and this was followed by *My Turn to Make the Tea* about her job as a reporter on a local newspaper in the 1950s.

Marriage in America was fictionalized as *No More Meadows*, while *Kate and Emma* was the result of her involvement with the NSPCC. Her lifelong love of horses and all animals produced fourteen children's books, one of which became the successful Yorkshire TV series, *Follyfoot*. *The Listeners* developed from her work with the Samaritans, and in 1974 she started the first Samaritan branch in America in Boston, Massachusetts, near Cape Cod where she lived for thirty-three years with her husband Commander Roy Stratton, US Navy.

She now lives in England in a thatched cottage on the Berkshire Downs. She has two daughters. Penguin have published her autobiography *An Open Book* and many of her other works including, most recently, *Enchantment*.

MONICA DICKENS

CLOSED AT DUSK

PENGUIN BOOKS

PENGUIN BOOKS

Published by the Penguin Group
Penguin Books Ltd, 27 Wrights Lane, London W8 5TZ, England
Viking Penguin, a division of Penguin Books USA Inc.
375 Hudson Street, New York, New York 10014, USA
Penguin Books Australia Ltd, Ringwood, Victoria, Australia
Penguin Books Canada Ltd, 2801 John Street, Markham, Ontario, Canada L3R 1B4
Penguin Books (NZ) Ltd, 182-190 Wairau Road, Auckland 10, New Zealand

Penguin Books Ltd, Registered Offices: Harmondsworth, Middlesex, England

First published by Viking 1990
Published in Penguin Books 1991
1 3 5 7 9 10 8 6 4 2

The lines quoted on p. 185 are from 'By the Wood' by Robert Nichols,
originally published by the Hogarth Press in the collection *Ardours and Endurances*.
Reproduced by permission of the Robert Nichols Estate

Printed in England by Clays Ltd, St Ives plc

Chapter One

'Keith!' No answer. 'Keith!' Rob came out of the playroom. 'I want you to help me – Keith! Where are you?'

The little boy ran along the corridor to Keith's door. 'You in there?' He opened the door, then went down to the next floor and opened several others, and banged and shouted outside a bathroom. Calling, he ran down the wide stairs and looked into the study, the sitting-room, the drawing-room, then a dash past the massed flowers in the hall to the dining-room. The table shone like a dark lake. The chairs waited politely. Keith's books and notebooks were scattered on the window seat.

'Keith!' Rob crossed the passage to the kitchen. Pans on the side of the Aga. Half a mug of coffee. Vegetables and the Chinese cleaver on the big table. The long striped apron not on the back of the door.

'Keith!' Rob called uncertainly down the basement stairs, and his voice disappeared into underground emptiness. He stood with his hand against the wall and listened. His heart was beating up under his chin. His chest struggled to get enough breath. His shout was weaker: 'Keith!'

Slowly, listening, he went down the stairs, keeping his shoulder against the wall. Keith must be in the cellar, getting potatoes. Any moment, his bare feet would come padding back on the cold stone floor. But Rob couldn't wait. He must find

Keith now, or break apart because he had been left alone in the house.

'Keith?'

On the worn green lino of the bottom step, at the edge of panic, he made himself lean round the end of the staircase to look down the dim vaulted tunnel of the basement, where light came meanly through dirty crescents of glass high up, and all the dark doors were closed on cells full of horrors.

'Keith! Keith!' With his arms out sideways, Rob ran through the tunnel in a blind panic for the door at the far end. His screams and sobs clamoured back at him off the walls. He was abandoned. Done for. This was what death was.

Gasping, he fought with the big key, somehow dragged open the heavy door and stumbled up the overgrown steps into dazzling sunlight.

People were walking about on the lawns, and bending over the flower beds. Rob stopped short, confused by the shocking difference between the immediate terror indoors and the peaceful unreality out here, then ran full tilt, wailing, down the slope and into a man and woman sitting on a rug on the grass.

'Here – steady on.' The child had knocked over Faye's plastic cup. Frank Pargeter stood up and caught the little boy's arm as he recovered himself and tried to run on towards the lake.

'What's the matter?' The boy was about six or seven, senseless with fear and tears. 'Are you lost?'

The child shook his head. He was shivering, his long skinny legs emerging from brief grubby shorts.

'Lost your mum?' No. 'Did you come here with someone?' The slobbery lower lip disappeared behind the large front teeth. 'By yourself?' No answer. Frank looked round for a gardener's cottage, or any other houses except the great turreted fortress. 'Show me the way, lad. I'll take you home.'

'Don't expect *me* to go, Frank,' Faye said redundantly. She unscrewed the top of the Thermos and poured herself the last of the tea.

The child led Frank round the side of the house where the bottom of the broad turrets swelled out like elephants' feet, and across the wide arc of gravel to the high front steps, where he stopped.

'Which way?'

'I don't want to go in.' The boy spoke for the first time, huskily, his voice still choked with tears.

'Here? You live here?' He was such a shabby, desolate little boy.

'I'm staying with Keith. My mother's in London.'

'Where's Keith?'

'I don't know!' The child began to wail again.

'How do we get in?' The double front doors were massive. They looked as if there were an iron bar behind them. 'Isn't there a side entrance or a garden door?'

'They're probably locked because of the visitors.'

'Come on.' Frank took him up the front steps. The boy could not reach the bell, so Frank pressed it and heard it ring far away.

'No one there.' The child looked piteously up at Frank from under his tangle of dark hair.

'They wouldn't leave you alone.'

'They did.'

Frank rang again twice, then took the boy round some walls and outbuildings and through a cobbled yard to where an old ladies' club was having cream teas in part of the stables.

'Hullo, Rob. Come for a cake?'

Swift as a hedgerow animal, the boy darted round the end of the tea-room counter and buried his distressed head in the woman's flowered skirt.

'What's up?'

'He was lost,' Frank offered.

'Lost? What rubbish. What game's this? Here, come on, Keith will be looking for you.' The woman went towards a door at the back of the room.

'Should I come too?' Frank was edging round the counter, wanting to see something of the impressive house. And what if there really was no one there?

'He's all right. Thank you.' The woman had a warm, reassuring smile.

Faye had got tired of sitting on the grass and had wandered away to censure the unruly tufts of thyme and thrift ranging over the flagstones of the terrace above the lawn. She would have had them out in a flash and made Frank concrete the cracks.

He looked across the beautiful still lake to the trees that crowded up one side of the long slope to where the wild part of the garden started. Faye had agreed to an outing in this wonderful May weather, and he had brought her here in the hope of investigating the thicket beyond the top of the hill, which, as a birdwatcher, he had spotted as a promising breeding area when he came here before, driving the minibus for the Venture Club. But Faye did not want to walk up the hill, and she did not want to be left like a bump on a log while Frank did. She wanted to go back to the car.

Frank picked up the *Guide to The Sanctuary Gardens* and his cardigan, which she had left on the grass, and set off slowly to find Faye. As he walked along the wide terrace in front of the house, he looked up at the rows of tall, clean windows, which regarded him calmly and frankly. The child must be all right. No cruel secrets here.

The *Guide* told him:

Closed at Dusk

The house which stands in these beautiful gardens, is not open to the public. It has been the home of the Cobb family since 1750, when Sir Desmond Cobb, successful farmer and agricultural advisor to King George II, replaced the sixteenth-century manor farmhouse with this magnificent dwelling designed by a pupil of John Wood the Younger.

In 1870 Sir Desmond's descendant Walter Cobb and his wife Beatrice changed the name of the house from Lynnford Place to The Sanctuary, in keeping with their mission to promote here the welfare and understanding of all living creatures. Most of the animal statues to be seen about the estate date from that time.

After a period of neglect during and after the Second World War, the magnificent gardens and lake have been restored and improved by Walter Cobb's great-grandson, William Taylor, the present owner, who welcomes you to The Sanctuary.

Open 2 pm April–October, Tuesday–Sunday and bank holidays. May–September: closed 6 pm. April and October: closed at dusk.

'I couldn't find you.' Rob climbed on to his stool at the kitchen table, blind with self pity.

'I was here. What's the panic?'

'I was calling and calling.'

'Of course.' Keith was chopping vegetables. 'You call me, call me all day long. "Keith, help me do this. Keith what's this? Why's this? Where are you?" I get fed up with it, so sometimes I don't answer.'

'When will Mummy be back?'

'Soon, thank God.'

Keith, who was Rob's mother's cousin, had been ill. In his second year at Cambridge, his will and energies had been undermined by a vague indisposition that made it increasingly hard to study or take exercise or stay up late.

'Psychosomatic.' Doctor John 'Unready' Reddy, family friend, harassed by a waiting-room full of old bodies stricken by winter-kill, could find nothing wrong. 'Something bothering you?'

'Lazy.' His mother, Harriet, and his older sister laughed, because they knew old Keith, always one to duck work if he could. Scared of failure, probably, after his disappointing first year. 'Brace up old lad,' his father said. 'You'll be all right.'

But when Keith had to drop helplessly out of *Three Ring Circus*, the annual student musical, his love, his baby, the focus of his college life, they did send him to a specialist, who knew about myalgic encephalomyelitis. ME: a set of horribly debilitating symptoms following a virus infection. It had attacked his central nervous system with devastating results. Six months off became nine months. He had missed playing and singing not only in that year's *Circus*, but in the one this year. Life in ruins, musical career a flop, cut off before it started.

After gradually crawling back to life from a hell of pain and weakness and general non-functioning gloom, he was spending the summer with Uncle William, his mother's brother. He worked outdoors in the huge garden and read and slept, to get his strength back before starting university again with people who had still been at school when he was a freshman. He was often tired, bored and peevish, and irritated now to be left for two days in charge of nervy, clamorous Rob. Ignoring the child's calls, hiding in the larder, was not cruelty – just a sick sort of joke for diversion, which he regretted now that Rob was on his stool at the kitchen table stuffing peanuts into his tear-swollen face.

'What's that going to be?' Rob made the grimace of ultimate disgust with which he greeted exotic food, or any unusual treat.

'*Tzu sat jing* with chicken *kung po*. I'm going to try it on us tonight and perfect it for the family.'

'If it's Chinese, I don't want it.'

'Starve then.'

'Why can't Ruth or Brenda come up? I never heard of a man cooking.'

'Your mother's men aren't that sort.'

'What men? She hasn't got any.'

'News to me.'

Ruth Barton came up in her flowered skirt and white apron to get the last batch of scones from the warming oven. She did some of the tea-room baking in her own house in the village, and some in this kitchen, which had been built in a corner of the raised ground floor in the 1930s, when no one would put up with the vast old draughty cavern in the basement, nor carry any more wide-armed trays up the back stairs when the dumb waiter stuck again.

'Too much garlic.' Ruth nodded at Keith's pungent chopping pile.

'I told you.' Rob sided with her eagerly.

'I thought you'd be outside, Keith. John Dix and Mac are off in the pine wood. There's only Stuart about to answer questions.'

One of Keith's jobs was to assist the visitors, with the knowledge that he had picked up from his Uncle William, and from working with the gardeners this spring and summer.

'I felt faint.'

'Rubbish, dear. You're supposed to be cured.'

'You don't get "cured" of ME. It lurks in the background. Big crowd today, Ruth?'

'Not too bad. Just as well, because Doreen's not been much help to me in the tea-room. Been – *you* know.'

'Psychic spells?'

Ruth shook her head and made a tight mouth. It was not supposed to be discussed in front of the highly strung little boy.

'Did she hear something?' Rob asked, half fearful, half thrilled.

Doreen was the only person who had heard the terrible sounds of the Connemara mare trapped with her colt fifty years ago when the wooden foaling box behind the stables had burned down. It had not been rebuilt. Part of that end of the stables, hosed clean of ancient horse smells and painted, was now the tea-room, extended by a porch, with tables on the cobbles and flowers in tubs and hanging baskets. In the scullery store-room, Doreen, with the pretty china in the sink, claimed to have heard an echo of the dreadful screams.

'She wouldn't have if she'd never been told about it.' Ruth tipped the scones off the baking tray and went to the short stairs that led down through winding rear passages to the tea-room.

Keith said darkly, 'When she first heard it, she *hadn't* been told.'

'That's nonsense.' Ruth gave Rob one of her best Ruth smiles, everything dimpling into comfortable curves, spaniel-brown eyes cushioned in crinkles.

That evening, after the chicken *kung po*, which was as weird as Rob had expected, he became nervous as it grew dark. He did not want to go up to his little cabin bedroom on the nursery floor.

'There's nothing to be scared of.'

'This house is too big.'

'It hasn't grown. You've known it since you were born.'

'I didn't know it was too big then.'

'Come on.' Because he remembered his own childhood terrors, Keith said, 'Let's go for a little tour and you'll see it's just its same old safe self.'

Delaying Rob's bedtime, they went all over the house with the dogs, switching on lights and leaving them on, so that The

Sanctuary seemed to blaze with life, as if the great house were full of excited people for Christmas.

Rob refused to go down to the basement, so they visited the larder and store-rooms and the serving pantry where the dumb waiter used to come up – 'Is the door locked? Show me it's locked,' because something ghastly might come up from underground – and the china pantry with the endless dresser and cupboards, then through the warm garlic climate of the kitchen and into all the ground-floor rooms.

The long drawing-room ran from front to back of the house with a deep five-sided bay at each swelling turret, two fireplaces, and the piano covered in family pictures.

'Pull the curtains.' Anything could be looking in from the dark outside: left-over visitors, robbers, kidnappers, wraiths of animals that had died here, Hardcastle from the mausoleum.

'Not worth drawing curtains just to be pulled back in the morning.'

With a flourish of an imaginary tailcoat, Keith sat down on the piano stool, tapestried long ago by his grandmother Sylvia as an imprisoned girl, and played one of the songs he had intended for *Three Ring Circus*.

> '*Time gone by . . . played a game.*
> *I'd be leader. All would follow.*
> *Look round now. No one there.*
> *Fingers click on empty air.*
> *Life? It's hollow.*'

'More, Keith.'

'Only if you'll sing.' Rob shook his head. 'Up then.' Keith pretended to bang the piano lid down on his own fingers, and cried like a clown, his eyes triangular behind the round glasses that were too big for his narrow face.

With the dogs going ahead, Charlotte hopping from stair to

stair, Corrie the labrador padding weightily, they explored some of the many bedrooms and bathrooms. When he could sidetrack Keith no longer, Rob followed him up to the nursery floor with the lagging tread of doom, because he knew he would not be allowed downstairs again.

'All right now,' Keith told him. 'Nothing ever happened up here.'

Where then? Where did something terrible happen downstairs?

Keith would not bother with the bedrooms and the little nanny's kitchen and the playroom where Rob kept the box of pipes and joints that his grandfather had given him when the old boiler-house was demolished. Rob was interested in pipes. He was inventing a way to drain the path that crossed the marsh garden at the far end of the lake.

The attic store-rooms were safely shut away behind a locked door at the end of the white-painted nursery corridor. The turret wing and passage where servants used to sleep was now closed off as a flat for the head gardener and his wife. But the housemaid's closet . . .

'Just open the door a tiny bit, Keith.'

'I won't.'

'I won't go to bed.' Rob sat down on the floor with his legs stuck out.

'Damn you, Robert.'

'Please.'

'Brat.' Keith opened the door with a swift flourish and switched on the light before Rob would open his eyes to risk a look at Flusher.

In the innocent room of ironing boards and drying rails and the dressing-up trunk and blankets stored on shelves with ski clothes, Flusher was a dreadful thing. It squatted in a corner by the sink, a very old, round toilet bowl with no seat but a porcelain draining board set into each side. Above it, a pull chain hung from a high cistern with embossed lettering: 'The Flusher, patent 1882'.

Why were all the children bewitched by this ugly relic of chamber-pot days and nights?

'Were *you*?' Rob asked Keith.

'Of course. We all were. Partly for a joke, like you.'

It wasn't a joke.

The cabin had been fitted up for a bygone naval cadet, to make him feel at home when he came on leave. It was just big enough for the high bunk with drawers underneath and a shallow fitted cupboard and shelves.

Kneeling on the pillow, Rob looked out of the window which had two bars, like all the windows on this floor. Oblongs of light lay on the circle of drive and the grass beyond. One of them lit up the crouching stone bulldog on top of the square pillar in the boundary wall.

'Lie down, Rob.'

'I can't. I'll get cot death.'

'What on earth are you talking about?'

'A boy at school's brother died of it. You lie down to sleep and then you die.'

'Boloney.' Keith switched off the corridor light, to make Rob yell out, 'You said you'd leave it on!' Keith switched it on again and went downstairs, laughing like Dracula.

Struggling out from beneath the limp weights of Charlotte and Corrie, Rob knelt again at the window and saw the oblongs of light go out one by one, and the bulldog disappear into thick darkness. Whatever had been waiting out there beyond the light drew closer. Rob wriggled back into the tunnel of bedclothes and listened for Keith's bare footsteps coming up the stairs. They came at last, pad, pad, wearily. *What if it wasn't Keith?* The footsteps passed his door. The labrador snored. Keith's bedroom door opened and shut, and his music started quietly.

Chapter Two

When Rob's mother Tessa arrived from London, she found him in the kitchen, dropping lemon biscuit dough neatly on to baking trays for Ruth.

'Where you been, where have you been?' He dropped the spoon on the floor and ran to Tessa.

'You know I've been at a conference.'

'I thought you would never come!'

'No you didn't,' Ruth said. 'You told me she was coming this morning.'

Rob did not feel shamed. It was only a ritual. He went out with his mother to find where Keith was working.

None of the gardeners had seen him for the last hour. They shrugged their shoulders and went on with what they were doing. Keith worked in spurts, for apprentice wages. He was a bit of a joke to them.

'Let's try the hidden garden.' Tessa made the playful secret face that used to be only for Rob and his father, and now was only for Rob. They raced the dogs along the lake, and went round its narrow end where it met the little Lynn river, cutting under the road from the village.

On a low green mound the miniature temple of the Egyptian cat-goddess Bastet stood blazing white in the sun against its semi-circle of dwarf cypresses. '*Remember Gigi.*' There was a new card pinned inside one of the fluted wooden pillars among the faded photographs and curling *in memoriams* to visitors' cats.

Behind the aromatic cypresses they took the path between the giant beeches to a low doorway in a wall so overhung with honeysuckle and wisteria and crimson glory vine that you could not see the bricks. Standing upright again – Rob had ducked unnecessarily with his mother – they were in a charming little closed garden of odd-shaped flower beds and grass paths that rambled without pattern between box edgings. White seats fitted into corners. There was a sundial that said, 'Never Too Late for Delight', a goldfish pond with yellow iris, and a tiny thatched summer house. Pottery models of small animals sat or prowled among the flowers and bushes. Stone lizards and frogs rested along the rim of the pond.

New visitors fancied, when they found this pleasance, that they had stumbled on a secret place which was private to the family and their friends. 'Well, but the door's open and there's no one about ...' They sat in the summer house and on the white seats, and felt crafty and privileged. They did not know about the real hidden garden between the angle of the coach-house wall and the high hedge of rhododendrons, where the family had their own flower garden and swimming pool and comfortable furniture on suntrap flagstones. Because of the late May heatwave, Tessa's father had filled the pool early this year. She and Rob eventually found Keith there, in the cold blue water.

For looking after Rob for two days, Tessa had brought her cousin a beautiful peach-coloured shirt and a volume, bound in soft leather, of Rimbaud's poems.

'Was the Beast all right?'

'Divine.' Keith hung on the edge of the pool and tried to lick Tessa's wet toes. The small nails were varnished cherries.

'He can be an awful pest.' She laughed down at Keith. 'Always wanting attention and calling. It can drive you mad.'

'Oh, no, he didn't do that.' Keith tilted back his head and squinted at Rob along the side of his bony nose.

Rob had put on his swimming trunks in the pool house. He did a spectacular jump into the shallow end. 'Race you a width,' he gasped at the surface.

'Too cold. Going back to work.' Keith tried to pull himself up, failed, and climbed out by the steps. He picked up his towel, and Tessa went with him to the door that led to the private walk behind the stables.

'Mummy – stay! Stay here and watch me swim – Mummy!' Rob took in water, and choked. But his mother was only standing laughing in the arched gateway, calling something to Keith as he went towards the house.

Rob had his mother to himself for two days before anyone else arrived. They did things that Tessa used to do here when she was a child, visiting Grandmother Sylvia. In the mornings before the visitors came, they waded in the marsh and rolled down the banks of the terraced lawns. She rowed him in the blue dinghy under the humped wooden bridge to the front of Walter Cobb's empty tomb, set into a high overgrown bank of the lake.

'I won't look.' Rob turned his head away. He did not mind seeing the mausoleum from the other side of the lake, but staring close up, you might see the heavy doors bulge and buckle, and the desperate spirits of hell burst out and blaze down the broken marble steps to set the lake on fire.

'There's nothing there, silly,' Tessa said. 'It's a good place.'
'*She put him there.*'
'For love. Your great-great-great-grandfather. She buried him here for love, with a statue of his favourite dog above, to guard him. Like Charlotte guards us.'

Tessa's rag-bag mongrel was in the bow of the boat, small

blunt head up, ears out sideways, short legs braced. Since she left Rex a year ago, Charlotte and Rob were the best things in Tessa's life. Rex had broken her heart, but she had never lost her buoyant optimism. By nature impulsive and disordered, she did not tie herself to future plans, but embraced whatever came along. She was at the moment a personnel counsellor with Maddox Management, a consultancy which ran seminars for business and professional staff. The sessions she conducted were lively and stimulating. Thanks to some inspired training with the great Dr Oscar Ferullo, she was equipped to help men and women improve working relationships. Their private lives might be a mess, but then so was Tessa's.

She tied up the boat for their picnic, and when visitors began to straggle into the gardens, they went back to the house.

Rob ran with his head ducked, as if he were naked. Tessa walked, and waved and smiled at people and said hullo. Some were pleased to see one of the family. Some were baffled, wondering about this friendly young woman in shorts, with her caramel hair gathered randomly on top of her head.

Tessa and Rob went down to the lodge cottage where Ruth's mother Agnes lived with Ruth's grandmother, Mary Trout, who was almost ninety. Troutie, as she had been to the family for as long as anyone could remember, sat in her big old fusty chair beside the window, so that she could observe cars and walkers going up and down the drive.

Starting at The Sanctuary as a fourteen-year-old under-maid before the First War, she had progressed to being nurse to Tessa's father and his brother and sister, and later cook and everything else to their mother. After Sylvia Taylor died and her son William restored the house and opened up the gardens, he wanted his beloved Troutie to help Ruth to start the tea-room. Non-feudal Agnes urged her to break free, but Troutie simply expanded her output of victoria sponges and bakewell tarts while her wrists and back held out, and continued to hobble up to the big house to mend clothes and polish silver for as long as she could walk.

Tessa kissed her. The old cheek was like a cobweb. 'Here's Rob, Troutie, you remember? My little boy.'

'She knows *that*.' Agnes's voice, relentless as the rooks, came from the other room.

'She knows everything.' Tessa toured the room to inspect once more the photographs of people with horses, horses without people, Beatrice Cobb bottle-feeding a baby lamb, Sylvia Taylor in a hideous hat, with a goat, William and Matthew in long school shorts, on donkeys; groups, weddings, babies; a Dutch china dog pulling a cart, glass birds from Venice, painted teacups – all the trophies of trips abroad brought back for someone who had never been abroad. 'Tell Rob some more about the old days, like you used to tell me. What do you think about?'

'What can she think about?' Agnes answered for her mother. 'At that age, it's a blank. Very peaceful. I can't wait.'

'I think about the good old times.' The long old-lady hairs waved as Troutie's toothless jaw moved to talk. Why didn't Agnes pull them out? Tessa did not like to suggest it. Rob watched from a safe distance, rubbing a fat china cat against his cheek. 'Such times we had with all the staff. I was only a little mite of twelve.'

'Fourteen,' from Agnes.

'First proper home I ever had. Never had a home like The Sanctuary. It was lovely.' Her voice quavered off.

'How could it have been?' Agnes came into the sitting-room in her purple jacket, a cigarette on her lip. 'That nasty basement with those terrible icy rooms. You ever seen the room where they washed out mops and cloths in cold water?' she asked Tessa. 'The tears froze on her face. Ma's told me. Who do you think it was found Maryann Button hanging from a rope at the back of the cellar where they hung the game?' Rob turned round from the army of ornaments on the mantelpiece. 'My mother, that's who. She was fifteen.'

'What games?' Rob asked.

'Hares, pheasants, partridge.'

'They hung up the birds?'

'It's all right, Rob.' Tessa made a face at Agnes.

'And Maryann Button with 'em.' Agnes had had a drink or two.

'They hung up the birds *alive*?'

'Come on, Rob.' Tessa put her arm round him. 'We must go, darling Troutie.' She raised her voice because the old woman had closed her eyes.

'Go and get down a hare,' Cook says. Behind the small furred corpses hanging from the beam, Maryann Button dangles from a gammon hook in her parlourmaid dress and white apron, the cap tipped forward on the skewed surrendered head, a pickling jar broken by the chair she has kicked over on its side.

'Clumsy to the last.' Phyllis Bunby sticks out her thick bottom lip before her face collapses and she sobs and slobbers for half an hour.

William and Dorothy Taylor came home on Thursday evening. When he turned the car into the drive under the two wrought-iron lambs that pranced together above the gateway, William smiled and said, 'There it is.'

'You always say that.' Dorothy had known that he would. 'Are you afraid that one day it won't be there?'

'I can't ever quite believe it's ours.'

The house had been built by one of William's ancestors to impress guests and neighbours with a sort of domesticated fortress. The walls were massive blocks of Cotswold stone, anchored at each corner by broad hexagonal turrets; and yet even on its most lowering days when it bulked darkly, lashed by rain against a hopeless sky, it was not grim and foreboding. Its size and weight were steadiness, and beauty was given to it by the harmonious slopes and angles of its many roofs, the elegantly placed chimneys, the calm ranks of Georgian windows, five panes high on the raised ground floor, four panes above, two under the roof, below the attic dormers.

'Your sister Harriet wants you to smother it with ivy and virginia creeper,' Dorothy said. 'She thinks it looks like a prison.'

In the turret ahead of them, sunset fire signalled from watery old glass. Oatmeal stone soaked up the glow.

'She can put her head in a bucket,' William said.

Growing up here, he had always adored this house, and now that it belonged to him in middle age, or he to it, he spent as much time here as he could, sleeping in the Chelsea flat only when he had to stay late in London.

William, a partner in a large firm of land agents, was fifty-five, a large rumpled man who was often taken for one of the gardeners, which pleased him. He was a hardworking, capable businessman, who could play at being sophisticated when necessary, but his likeable face was still boyish, his pleasures and enthusiasms vulnerably simple. His passion was this house and garden, which he had inherited twelve years ago when his mother died. His wife Dorothy, who had preferred their smaller home, had come to terms with The Sanctuary and its unending demands. With the battle finally won to repair the devastation of Sylvia Taylor's last eccentric years, Dorothy forgave the house and allowed it to make her comfortable, running it with the same energy and competence she brought to all her work. She was a child psychologist. At fifty-seven, she saw private and NHS patients at a local clinic and was consultant to a children's home and the area fostering service, as well as giving some time to a support group for single parents in London.

She was small and purposeful; William was overgrown and careless. Now that her hair was grey, she kept it short and close to her head, her eyes, under the abrupt fringe, still a clear and startling light blue behind rather severe rimless glasses.

William loved her deeply with the love of years. He was proud of her, although felt some regret that she had grown less womanly as her children grew away from her; but Dorothy had never much cared for her more yielding maternal self. She was satisfied with her self-sufficient middle age.

William went straight round the side of the house to check his seedlings in the alpine house. Tessa and her mother laid cheek against cheek.

'Hullo, Mum. How's Tantrum Tactics?'

'Very good. How was your conference?'

'All right, I hope. Bit tricky, a diversified publishing group. They seem to have been conducting a hidden war, with four different sides.'

'So I suppose you told them to fire all the cannons, Tessa, beat each other up, say terrible things no one will ever forget?' Dorothy's problem children could say anything they wanted. For grown-ups, she favoured self-control.

A reliable granny, she had brought books and a convertible monster for Rob. Wum (the first grandchild had called him that after seeing William spelled Wm) had brought some grey plastic elbow joints he had found in a skip in Flood Street.

Rob was allowed to start his night on the couch in the study. Keith cooked the Chinese meal, then was tired and went to bed early. When he picked up the dead weight of Rob asleep and sweating gently, he could only carry him to the halfway landing. His Uncle William, almost three times his age, took the sleeping child from his arms and carried him easily up to the cabin room.

Chapter Three

On Friday, William Taylor's brother Matthew came with his young daughter Nina, of the dusky impenetrable hair. Matthew, a professor of English at a provincial university, was broader and shorter than William, greyer and balding, although he was a few years younger. His wife had died of cancer two years ago when Nina was twelve.

Tessa's older brother Rodney came with his wife and three children and two King Charles spaniels. Everybody brought their dogs to The Sanctuary. Rob's mother went into high gear when her brother arrived, as if she had not had any fun with anyone of her own generation for weeks. After tennis, everyone swam, and Tessa fooled about gaily and paraded her body, although it was only family. Keith watched her and bit his nails. Rodney, who strove to be a good father because he was away a lot, as an international banker, challenged his son Dennis to races and diving contests. Rob sulked and would not put on his swimming trunks.

'Where's *your* father these days?' Nina asked Rob. With a torn man's shirt over her swimsuit, she was reading by the pool with the eye that was not concealed by hair. 'This family – I can't keep up.'

'My mother got sick of him, so he married another person. Where's your mother anyway?'

Nina grunted.

'Is she dead? I forgot.'

After the Closing Bell had rung from the tall cypress tree, the visitors were gone and the window of the little ticket hut was shuttered up, the family had drinks on the terrace while the sun went down. Upstairs in the playroom, Rob had failed to frighten his cousin Annabel with a story about The Flusher, but her brother Dennis offered to tell him something so much worse, something so horrible . . .

'I won't listen! Mummy!' he screamed out of the window. Tessa waved back at him gaily.

'I wish the Sterns weren't coming,' William said at breakfast. 'Much rather garden all day.' He had been outside with the dogs since 6.30, tying up the clematis shoots rampaging along the front balustrade of the terrace. 'Wish I hadn't invited them.'

'Why did you?' Dottie was in a neat pair of overalls, ironed as well as clean. She was going to paint the windowsills in the library.

'I need him. Sir Ralph is a hot number since he made that speech about the dollar at the CBI dinner. He seems to know everybody . . . he can get me to a group of rich felons I want to talk to about this big land purchase at Chard, and developing an equestrian centre.'

He sighed. He resented even thinking about business on a day like this. Sir Ralph Stern, an inflated power broker, would descend as from a higher plane, hoping to impress this peaceful family as much as he impressed himself, and he would want to have closed policy sessions with William, shut up in his study with the whisky decanter.

Lady Stern would be too elegant and social, affronted to find nobody special invited to dinner. She would aerate the lawn with high heels and pretend to recognize the waterfowl.

She turned out to be quite charming. Sir Ralph got out of the Bentley, his predictably imposing self: fat nipples under a silky polo neck, tan hacking jacket, oxblood riding boots. His wife held out both hands to William and would have kissed Dorothy, with any encouragement.

'I'm Angela,' she said. 'We met briefly at the Mandersons', do you remember? Probably not. But I didn't forget what you told me about The Sanctuary.'

She greeted Keith and the children enthusiastically and with respect, and gave them appropriate small gifts. She had bothered to find out from William's secretary who would be here. She ran her hands through her frosted yellow hair and dropped her embroidered jacket carelessly on a chair in the hall before going straight through the glass doors to the terrace to see the lake and garden. Tessa took a look at the jacket label.

Angela swam before lunch, graceful and ripe, with firm limbs and a bloom on her skin. Although it was another amazing May day, Sir Ralph would not swim. As expected, he cornered his host, and they talked about his recent business book, *Games of Chance*, which William had bought after he invited him for the weekend.

At a quarter past two, Sir Ralph looked out of the wide dining-room window and said, 'Good God, you are being invaded.'

'Time to worry, if we weren't.'

'How can you stand these people charging all over your property . . . spying on you?'

Two women were passing along the top lawn between the terrace and the lake. Seeing people behind the distant dining-room window, one of them waved cheerfully.

'The garden is financed by a family trust which Matthew and I manage. We couldn't keep the garden up without the visitors.' William had told him this already.

'I couldn't stand it,' Sir Ralph said, as if he had not heard.

Tessa took him off to see the standing stones at Avebury, although he would object to the crowds on a Saturday. Dottie, who had presided over the cold lunch still in her overalls, with specks of paint on her glasses, went back to the library window-sills, trailed by the whiskery grey dog who had come here as a stray and attached himself to her, although she showed him no consideration. She had named him Folly, for picking her, and usually addressed him as Fool.

When Angela Stern offered to help, Dottie said, not rudely, but honestly, 'I like to work by myself.'

Angela said agreeably, 'Good, because I didn't really want to.'

What she wanted was to put on a striped sundress and plunge out to explore the gardens with William.

Some people with classic views about the relationship of building and landscape felt that the plethora of animal sculpture at The Sanctuary was too quaint and sentimental for the uncompromising bulk of the house. But Angela was enchanted with the legacies of Walter and Beatrice Cobb.

'When they inherited the house', William said, 'they renamed it The Sanctuary, because that was what they wanted it to be for all living things. After their death, their eldest son Frederick was interested in the gardens, I believe, but it was his wife, my tyrannical grandmother Geraldine Cobb who ran the show.

'Their son was killed in the First War, so their daughter Sylvia, my mother, stayed on here after she married my father. Matthew and I and Harriet, Keith's mother, were brought up at The Sanctuary.'

With the labrador Corrie, named after the buttery coreopsis 'Sunshine' that would soon gleam in clumps all down the long border, and her bounding year-old son, they visited the animal statues. Angela examined with eyes and hands the stone bull-dog watching the front door and the mastiff on the ivied mound, broad head laid along strong paws to point towards his master's tomb. On the side of his stone slab was carved his testimonial: 'Faithful unto Death'. William showed her the rearing wild pony on its pedestal at the entrance to the stable yard, the delicate French deer at the edge of the copse, the birds, the little field and woodland animals among the shrubs and flowers.

Many of them had been discoloured and damaged when William began to renew The Sanctuary twelve years ago, restoring the gardens to much more than their former glory. He had scrubbed the statues clean and had some of them repaired by a young local sculptor. For the birth of Dennis, the first grandchild, William had commissioned him to make a small biblical-looking donkey to stand by the swing tree.

In the temple of Bastet at the end of the lake, the cat that had crowned the free-standing central column had long ago been smashed by marauding children. William had buried the pieces respectfully, and had the sitting goddess remodelled as an unearthly short-haired Abyssinian with long front legs and a sphinx-like stare.

Angela hung about the little pillared temple for a long time, looking at the pictures and remembrance cards, and chatting to visitors about her own cats and theirs, while William, who always had secateurs or a knife in his pocket, culled dead heads from the *primula denticulata* on the bank at the edge of the lake.

'I love it, William.' She came and held out the wide skirt of her sundress for the dead flowers. 'If I send you last year's Christmas card picture of my tortoiseshells, will you put it up in the temple?'

'Bring it back yourself.'

She looked at him curiously, and he grinned. He was very taken with her.

Angela wanted to see the tomb of Walter Cobb, the mastiff's master, which was more easily approached from the water. William got the oars from a toolshed, and, as he was untying the blue dinghy, he heard a faint high pitched shout from across the lake. He looked up. Rob's head was poking through the bars of the playroom window. He was wailing, 'Wait for me, Wum!'

Some of the visitors looked up at the house and smiled. William put his hands to his mouth and called back, 'Hurry up!'

By the time William had pulled the boat out of the reeds and Angela was on board, looking round radiantly like Cleopatra in her barge, Rob came tearing down the opposite bank and over the wooden bridge in breathless agitation, head thrown back and mouth desperate, as if he were in the last gasps of the 200-metre dash.

'Welcome aboard,' Angela said, and dropped her voice ominously. 'We're cruising to the mausoleum.'

'I know,' Rob told her, 'but don't be afraid.'

They ducked to go under the humped white bridge. As they straightened up on the other side, a man in tank-tread hiking boots who came down the long slope from the copse stepped on to the bridge and raised a hand.

'Afternoon, Mr Taylor. Lovely day for a sail!'

'Hullo,' William called back. 'Nice to see you.'

'Who's that?' Angela asked.

'No idea. I must have seen him here before.'

'So have I,' Rob said. It was the man with the wild white hair who had taken him back to the house when he had run out of the basement door in terror.

'Casing the joint,' Angela said. 'What's he got in the green bag?'

'Duck poison,' Rob said.

'His lunch?'

'A bomb.'

'Don't scare me, Rob,' Angela said. 'My son used to terrify me when he was your age. Creeping up behind me and whispering, or hiding behind clothes in a cupboard and groaning when I opened the door. He thought it was funny.'

On the bank of the overgrown promontory where the mausoleum and the steps leading down to it were half buried, William held the boat, so that Angela could see the winged moulding on the lead doors and the legend under the pediment: 'Love is Eternal.'

'Who's in there?' Angela whispered. She thought that Rob, eyes round, bottom lip sucked behind his oversize front teeth, was only pretending fear.

'Nobody,' William said. 'Walter Cobb died when Beatrice was only about forty-five. She had this vault made and put him inside, so that from her bedroom window up there in the turret, where Dottie and I sleep, she could look out on him across the lake.'

'Tell about Hardcastle, Wum.'

'Are you supposed to know about that?'

'Mummy told me. Beatrice got a boy-friend, it was the vicar, and she and Hardcastle would look out of the bedroom window at my what-is-it – my great-great-great-grandfather alone out here in the moonlight.'

'It's thrilling.' Angela encouraged him. 'What happened then?'

'I forget.' Rob was suddenly out of his depth. He leaned over the side of the boat to pull at a water-lily leaf.

William said, 'The Reverend Hardcastle died, and she buried him here too.'

'They're still in there?' Angela was enthralled.

'Oh, no, her daughter-in-law was a gorgon who wouldn't

27

stand any nonsense like that. After Beatrice went to join her donkeys and shetlands in the Elysian fields, Geraldine sent the two blokes off to join her in the churchyard. They're not here.'

'*They are.*' Rob stood upright to tell Angela, 'If there's a moon tonight, *don't look out of the window.*'

'Thanks, I won't.'

As William rowed towards the marsh, Angela told Rob that her son Peter used to dress up in a sheet and stand gibbering in the headlights of cars bringing guests for dinner.

'He was a wild boy,' Rob said, with satisfaction. 'Did Sir Rollo – Sir Rufus – whack him?'

'Ralph isn't Peter's father. I was married to someone else then.'

William let the boat drift through shallow water into the soggy bank, and he and Rob got out and stood on the half-submerged boardwalk discussing conduits and sunk overflows.

'We'll talk to George Barton. He's good on drainage. Tell you what, Rob, bring your notebook down here tomorrow afternoon, and we'll draw up some plans to show him.'

When Rob ran back to the house, Angela said, 'You're a good grandfather, Wum.'

'I wish I were.'

'I like you. I knew I would.'

Did she look at every man like that, with dancing eyes and a waiting smile? William could only say, 'Let's go and get Ruth to give us some tea.'

He quite often joined visitors to have a cup of tea, but a coachload had come and there was no room inside, so he and Angela sat on upturned half-barrels in the courtyard. A few white fantails, descendants of the huge flock Beatrice and Walter had bred, pecked about on the cobbles. There were tubs of wallflowers. The tiles of the stable roofs were rosy in the sun. A trickle of people went in and out of the toilets, which used to be a harness room for the driving horses.

William went to ask Doreen for tea and cake, and after a wait, Ruth brought it out to them, her clear, no-nonsense face looking cross.

'She forgot,' she said. 'That woman. You should have asked me for it.'

'You've got enough to do.' William introduced Angela and Ruth summed her up. 'Still having trouble with Doreen?' he asked.

'Trouble?' Ruth rolled up her eyes. 'If she lasts out the summer, Mr Will, I won't.'

'She'll never leave.' William watched Ruth's broad flowered hips bustle back into the tea-room. 'She's everything here, helps in the house and the kitchen, runs this profitable little business. Her family has been here for ages. Place is her life.'

He was happy sitting across from Angela at the rough wooden table. A flicker of guilt led him to say, 'Ralph and Tessa are probably having a cream tea together at Avebury.'

Angela laughed.

'Why is that funny?' he asked her. 'It doesn't seem funny, you and me having tea here together. Seems a bit' – say it, William – 'romantic.'

She got up. Damn! He'd bust it. But she was only going to buy another piece of Ruth's fruit cake from the tea-room counter.

The air cooled down with the end of the day. They had drinks at the garden end of the drawing-room; from the big bay window they could see the startling whites and intense pinks holding the sun in the flower border, and the deepening colours of the lake.

Angela, devastating in black trousers and a wide white silk blouse gathered into a gold dog-collar, huge sleeves braceleted with gold, made Tessa, in bright cottons, feel like a dairymaid.

Angela went over to William to look at the crest on his blazer pocket. 'That was on the letter you sent with the map.'

'It's The Sanctuary symbol. Two of Beatrice Cobb's gambolling lambs. She used to take the runty ones the farmers would have let die and give them a proper chance at life.'

Ralph Stern took the opportunity to give a brief dissertation on the eighteenth-century farmers of Avebury, who had broken up many of the great sarsen stones for building.

'It's comforting to remember,' William said, 'that we're less destructive now.'

'Don't you believe it,' Ralph ordered. 'All those depressing tourists scattering iced-lolly wrappers – they don't give a damn.'

'You had a good time anyway?'

'Thanks to your daughter.' Ralph's indigo-lidded eyes feasted darkly on Tessa, vivid in her scarlet blouse and skirt splashed with poppies. 'I'm half in love with her.'

And I may be more than half in love with your wife, William thought. Stop that, you bloody idiot! He removed his eyes from Angela's white and gold brilliance and went out to the kitchen to get more ice.

Ruth Barton had closed the tea-room, put the cash in the safe and gone home to make supper for George and her teenage sons; now she had come back to help Polly Dix, the head gardener's wife, with the dinner.

'Said anything to Doreen yet?' William asked her.

'Till I'm blue in the face.'

'She won't change.' Polly was bland and blonde with a cushiony bosom and fat calves tapering into small feet in dirty trainers.

'Why not?' Ruth slapped some fish about in a dish of flour. 'I've given her every chance.'

'She likes herself like that.'

'The customers don't. She can be quite rude,' Ruth told William. 'Takes offence. She's very *sensitive*.' Being down-to-earth and unpretentious people, Ruth and Polly and William all made a face at that. 'She fusses and goes all spooky. Last week she wouldn't serve a man with an eye patch. She needs the money, but she won't come to work if she's upset, and I have to get young Brenda to help, or Polly to come down, with the twins.'

'Bloody nuisance,' William said. 'You'd better fire her. Find someone else. Talk it round, put something in the *Gazette*.'

'Is that what you want?'

'Do what you like.'

'You're the boss, Will.'

'No, you are.'

'Don't have me on.'

'I mean it, Ruth. It's your show. You hired her, you fire her.'

Rob had been whining round the drawing-room, trying to nag someone into playing snap.

'Play with me!'

'Not now.'

But ten-year-old Dennis had only to come wandering in and remark casually, 'Give you a game of cribbage if you like,' for Uncle Matthew to say, 'All right, old son. Just let me get another drink.'

Nina was lying on the carpet with her legs tangled in a long fusty skirt. Rob slumped down beside her and pulled the loose sweater sleeves back from her hands, so she could read to him.

'The children's hour.' Ralph Stern made the best of the fact that children were all over the place in the house – Rodney's wife Jill had just brought her baby down.

'Nice,' Angela said. 'Why didn't we have children?'

'You were too old.'

31

'Five years ago? I might have had a genius. People do, at forty.'

'You might have had another Peter.'

'The wild boy?' Rob looked up from the floor, remembering what he had heard in the boat.

'That's flattering him.' Ralph could be quite offensive to his wife, and her beloved son was an easy target; but she pretended not to notice. Polite and attentive to her husband, she had evidently decided to make this marriage work.

William was afraid she must have thought him quite silly in the tea-room courtyard.

Towards the end of a long, agreeable dinner, he looked down the table and raised his glass to his dear familiar Dottie, at ease in one of her neat, all-purpose dinner dresses, tiny pearl ear-rings, but no other jewellery, no make-up – untroubled, safe.

'All's well.' It was an age-old talisman between them.

Angela raised her glass too. 'I like this family. I love this house. Thanks, Ralph,' she gleamed down the table at him, 'for bringing me to The Sanctuary.'

He spread his hands, taking full credit.

When they left the table, a pitiful figure in Superman pyjamas was at the bottom of the stairs, huddled against the banisters.

'Rob!' Tessa swooped. 'My poor deprived child. Why didn't you come in to us?'

Cuddled, triumphant, Rob thought: Because this looks more pathetic.

'What's wrong, darling?'

'Cot death.'

'Oh, Rob – don't joke about things like that.'

'I dreamed about Flusher.'

'Who's Flusher?' Angela asked.

'Something terrible. I'll show you if you like.'

'Tomorrow.'

Tessa took the child upstairs, stayed with him until he was asleep, and came down to the chairs grouped comfortably round the drawing-room fire. Beyond the uncurtained windows at each end of the long room, a still, cool night enclosed the light and warmth.

'He's all right. He often comes wandering down in London.' Tessa sat down, and Charlotte, her little woolly dog, jumped into her lap. The yellow labrador lay dutifully by William's chair. A black cat slept on the hearth. Fool sat alert, watching Dottie from under his fierce brows as she moved about with the coffee.

'He works himself up,' Keith said. 'All the silly kids want to be spooked by Flusher.'

'So did we.' William remembered locking his brother in the housemaid's closet and being chastised by Troutie when she found Matthew in hysterics. 'Because there are no ghosts in this house, we have had to invent them.'

'But look here.' Ralph Stern had both hands reverently round a Victorian goblet, making a connoisseur's face at his brandy. 'There must be stories about real ghosts in a fantastic old place like this. Skeletons in cupboards, that sort of thing . . . grey ladies . . .'

'Yeah.' Keith laughed. 'Grandmother Sylvia. She holed up here for years, you know, with junk and old newspapers. Pretty weird lady.'

'She wasn't.' Dorothy gave him a look to shut him up. 'She simply felt safe here.' Sylvia was an eccentric myth now, her deficiencies towards her son William understood and forgiven, as far as Dottie was concerned.

'What about the lilies?' Keith used the enlarging lenses of his round glasses not only to see through, but to stare at you provokingly.

'Nothing about the lilies.'

'My mother told me.'

'Harriet's silly gossip,' Dottie said dismissively. 'There are no supernatural phenomena at The Sanctuary.'

'But if there *were*,' Ralph did not want it dismissed, 'what would they be? If this were a different kind of house, how would it be haunted?'

'You like that kind of stuff, Sir Ralph?' Rodney did not see the point of it, now that science and technology had left it far behind.

'Yes,' Ralph said. 'I must say I do. I'm –' self-deprecating laugh – 'I suppose you could say I'm a bit psychic.'

'Oh, darling, what nonsense.' Angela moved to sit on the floor and lean against his perfect trousers. One of her goodwill missions was to try to stop him bringing every subject round to himself.

'I mean,' he paid no more attention to her than he ever did, 'for instance, who would the ghost of Flusher be?'

Chapter Four

'Flusher,' said Nina solemnly, on the stool by the fire, hugging her knees, 'is not a ghost, actually. It's a domestic monster. It lives upstairs in a room called the housemaid's closet, and no child will ever go in there alone.'

'Except that dentist's child, do you remember, Neen?' Keith was playing up to his cousin. 'He thought it was a good place to hide, in Sardines.'

'Sheldon his name was, poor little boy.'

'What happened to him?' Ralph spoke seriously; the other grown-ups were smiling encouragingly at Nina, who had not talked much in company before her mother died, and hardly at all after.

She stared at the fire for a moment, then lifted her head and put back the heavy mat of hair with a small childish hand, to drone at him, 'He was never seen again.'

'Oh, come on,' Matthew said. 'No fairy-tales.'

'No.' Ralph raised an autocratic hand. 'Go on, Nina.'

'Well.' She took a breath and talked fast. 'Flusher is this really grotesque sort of ancient loo, right? With a sort of draining-board round the hole instead of a seat, where the poor overworked female slaves, right, had to empty and scrub out the chamber-pots.'

'And so?'

'So one of them, a slave, not a potty, right, was driven to

despair. She killed her baby, and then she –'

'Go on.'

'She flushed it away.'

'And ever since then,' Keith added with relish, 'Flusher waits hungrily for another meal.'

'Sheldon?' Angela whispered, bright rose lips parted.

'Who knows?' Nina wrapped her arms round herself and rocked her whole body back and forth on the stool.

'That's it.' Her grandmother held up a hand. 'That's enough, both of you.'

'All right.' With a swift change of mood, Nina scrambled to her feet and stamped to the door, knocking into a small table. 'I'll go to bed then, if I'm not wanted.'

Matthew moved uncertainly, as if he would go after her, then sat back and said shyly to Angela, 'Sorry about that.'

'Don't worry,' Ralph said. 'She's used to sulking bloody teen-agers.'

'Nina's mother,' Dottie told him politely, 'died less than two years ago.'

Angela, who had again ignored the sneer at her son, saved Ralph's bacon by asking him brightly. 'Want to hear another story, since you liked that one? Will told me about the poor pony mare and her colt that got burned to death, in the foaling stable. Local people said that you could hear the terrible screaming for years afterwards, and one of the women in the tea-room says she hears it now – she went home without washing up the cups.'

'Well, there you are.' Ralph was pleased with her. 'What else? I mean, I know,' he bowed to Dorothy, 'good Doctor Taylor, there are no ghosts at The Sanctuary, but this is such a pleasant evening and no one wants to go to bed. So let's go on pretending there are . . .'

'If there *was* a ghost here,' Rodney said, 'which there isn't, I suppose the wretched thing would have to be in the basement.'

'The basement, ah yes.' Ralph Stern, sophisticate of cellars and dungeons, nodded.

'We used to play torture chambers there as kids in my grandmother's day,' Rodney went on, 'and pretend we saw the spectre of Maryann Button, hanging among the pheasants and hares. Though I think Troutie made that up, don't you, Tessa?'

'No, Rod. She may not know the score now, but she still remembers old things like that. She remembers the All Souls night when someone broke into the mausoleum and tried to prise the stone slabs off the tombs of Walter and Hardcastle.'

'Body-snatchers?' Ralph Stern grinned. He did not smile enough, but when he grinned, you didn't want more.

'They never knew,' Tessa said. 'It might have been the dead men trying to get out.'

'Any dogs and cats rising up with eldritch howls from the pet cemetery?' Her sister-in-law's quick, crisp voice put Tessa among the silly children. 'You'll be putting that grotesque thing in there one of these days.' Jill's tight blond pony-tail wagged as she nodded at the little dog asleep in the chair against Tessa's thigh. 'You shouldn't let her up on chairs, you know. She's supposed to be a sporty little type with those shoulders and chest, not a lap dog. You spoil her.'

'I need her.' Tessa had been sleepy, after drinking a fair amount of wine at dinner and playing up to Ralph, just for general practice with older men, but she was awake now, and piqued. 'I love this funny-looking mongrel. People who live alone, or with just a small child, need a dog who thinks they're the best thing on earth. You married Rod out of your nursery, but you try living without a man, Jill, you just try it.'

'Your choice. You could have stayed with Rex.'

'Thanks.' Tessa made a face at her.

'Anyway, I got the idea you weren't exactly alone at the moment, Tessa. Who was that muscle man you had in tow at the theatre and didn't introduce to me?'

'Lenny? I wouldn't risk introducing *him* to any of you.'

The sisters-in-law were only sparring lightly, but Dorothy picked up Tessa's defensiveness, and asked, 'Why? When have we ever been critical?'

'You all were at first, with Rex.'

'Well,' William said mildly, 'he *was* rather heavily married.'

'He won you over, though. None of you waited till his divorce to fall in love with him.'

'Perhaps we should have followed our first instincts,' Dorothy said dryly. 'I'm sorry.' She turned to the Sterns with a civil smile. 'Just family chatter.'

Ralph, who had tuned out when the women started pecking at each other, said, 'About the lilies, Dorothy. You were going to tell us about the lilies.'

'I was not. I have no story to tell.'

'Matthew?' Ralph raised a dark Mephistophelean eyebrow at William's quiet brother, who shook his head.

'My turn.' Keith put a log on the fire and poked it into incandescence. Since his illness, he was often cold. 'I'm panting for my turn.'

'I thought you were too tired to pant.' Jill was one of the people who took myalgic encephalomyelitis with a grain of salt.

'I am, but I can lie in tomorrow, if you'll keep that baby quiet.'

'I'll bring her in for you to amuse.'

'I'll tell the story of the Reverend Hardcastle.' From the fireplace, Keith said to Ralph, 'Great-great-grandma Beatrice's lover. He had a beautiful tenor voice, for a parson. Much in demand at soirées, and he got a good choir going in the church. It broke up after he died, but I was told that when he was shacked up with Walter in the mausoleum, Beatrice opened her bedroom window one night and heard the non-existent choir singing, across the lawns and fields, with Hardcastle's soaring tenor.'

Leaning on the mantelpiece, head poked forward like a hanged man, Keith looked gloomily round his audience. Where had he unearthed this story?

'I never heard that before,' Dorothy said.

'That doesn't make it not true,' Keith said. 'Since Beatrice, certain switched-on souls also claim to have heard the choir.'

'Why not?' Sir Ralph had gone to the bay window to look out at the moonless garden, his head slightly turned, as if he were listening.

Keith went to the piano at the other end of the room and played a few bars of a chorale.

'Ralph!' Angela called sharply to her husband. 'Come away from the window. You're taking this game too seriously.'

'Anything is possible if we will only listen.' He turned round and looked at them with glittering eyes. 'Listen.' He put up his hand for silence. The others sat still and tense, and everyone jumped at the small click of the door handle. The door opened slowly, just an inch or two.

Rodney got up with an exclamation, and pulled it open.

Rob was there, very small in the high doorway.

Tessa got up swiftly and went to him, but he headed past her to the fire and climbed into the chair with Charlotte. Tessa sat down again and took him on to her lap, his hot head under her chin, the pressure of his bony damp body all that her breast wanted.

The others were getting up. The evening was over. The stories were done.

'So I was right.' Ralph Stern was his usual bumptious self

now, not mysterious. 'Many phantom memories to haunt a strange old house.'

'Sorry,' William said. 'Nothing sinister or strange – unless peace and happiness is strange. There's a smaller ring of stones, you know, above Avebury, where the ancients celebrated joy in life. They called it The Sanctuary. That's where this place gets its name.'

'I know,' Ralph said, predictably. He didn't.

'Was I stuffy with him?' William asked Dottie, through the open door of their old-fashioned bathroom, where she was scouring her small healthy teeth. 'I got sick of him playing spooks with our honest old house. Do you think he's really psychic?'

'He was putting it on.' Dottie came to the doorway in her seersucker pyjamas, polishing her face on a towel. 'For control. To be different from the rest of us: "I know something you don't know." Tiresome man. I'm sorry for his wife.'

'So am I.' All day and evening William had been stirred by rescue (and other) fantasies. 'I wish I didn't have to go on seeing him, but he's setting up a meeting for me with the Barrett Mayne people. Dinner at his house. Will you come?'

'No,' Dorothy said, and William's foolish heart leaped ahead to excitement.

Dottie had been losing interest in sex as her fifties advanced. She was not interested tonight.

'Some psychologist,' William grumbled. 'You're bored with it, so I'm supposed to be too.'

'Don't be childish, Will.'

'If I were a child, you would understand my case.'

She turned away from him and lay neat and straight, the back of her small cropped head, the short strong neck above the innocent rounded pyjama collar, touching and familiar. 'Anyway, too much wine and whisky, Wum.'

'You're right.' First he was a child to her, then a grandfather. He lay for a while, thinking about Angela in the big puffy guestroom bed with Mephistopheles. Then he masochistically started on another chapter of Ralph Stern's obviously ghosted book, *Games of Chance*. He fell asleep with the light on, mouth open, book on the floor, where the yellow labrador snored.

'No nightmares?' William, up first, was in the kitchen when Angela came down in a crimson kimono, looking for coffee.

'I slept like an angel in that heavenly bed.'

Sitting companionably at the table with him, Angela sighed and said, 'I feel comfortable here, Will. What was the toast you gave your wife at dinner?'

'All's well.'

'You're lucky.' She put a hand on his arm.

'Isn't it for you?'

But she had taken the hand away and put it round her orange juice. Dennis and Annabel came charging down the hall with their father, and that was it.

Rodney's family left soon after breakfast, because he was flying to New York in the evening. William went to inspect fences and a cracking wall with George Barton, who could put his hand to anything. When William came round from behind the hidden garden, Angela was in the cat temple. She had found a small picture of her tortoiseshell cats in her wallet, and was pinning it up among the other love tokens. 'Aren't you coming back with the Christmas card photograph then?'

'I'll give it to you at Ralph's high-powered dinner.'

'I wish you'd bring it here.' Steady, William.

Her eyes laughed into his. 'Perhaps I could get Ralph to bring one of his horrible tycoons to The Sanctuary.'

The hell with that, William longed to say. I want *you*.

A reminder of sanity, Dottie and Rob were pottering about

in wellingtons with hammers and nails, repairing one of the duck platforms. Male menopause, said Grandpa Wum's inner clown.

Angela went to help Tessa get lunch ready. 'Nothing very grand, I'm afraid. We have to clear off the terrace at two, like Cinderella.'

'Or charge extra to see the Taylors' feeding time. Are you –' Angela paused, chopping celery for chicken salad, then finished impulsively, 'are you all right?'

'Yes, of course. Why not?'

'Your father told me you'd had a dodgy time.'

'Well, I did. Just desserts. Meet fabulous man. Go insane for him. Seduce him away from adoring wife. Five years later, I'm – sane, I suppose. I see this bullying faker in the cold light of reason, and get out before he can hurt me any more.'

'What was the wife like?'

'Never seen her. Sort of flat and beige, I think. They married too young, and he went onward and she didn't. A beige bitch, Rex used to say. Beige and barren. God knows what he said about me to all the other women.'

'You poor child.'

'Don't give me that. I'm thirty-one. I knew what I was doing, and I know what I'm going to do now – take care of myself, enjoy my life, as I always have.'

'I'm glad.'

'No, I'm ruthless and selfish, haven't they told you?'

'They love you.'

'In spite of. Yes.' Tessa gathered her tumbling hair on top of her head with both hands, then let it fall and stretched out her arms with a serene smile, 'Isn't it great about families?'

When everyone was sitting round the terrace table, Keith came out in frayed khaki shorts, his narrow chest bare.

'Telephone, Sir Ralph. Your secretary.'

'I knew it.' Angela picked up a chicken wing and bit into it. 'Now we'll have to leave.'

In a few minutes, Ralph came out again with a face like death.

'My God,' his wife said, 'have we lost a fortune?'

'Come inside, Angela.'

Angela's son Peter had been killed in a car crash in the West Country.

While they packed hastily, William went to bring round the Bentley. It was after two. A group of visitors crossing the end of the gravel sweep watched curiously as Ralph, grim, and Angela, looking smaller, came out of the front door, Matthew carrying their bags.

'Let me drive you up,' William offered. 'I can get a train back.'

But Ralph was in charge. He started off fast, scattering gravel; Angela turned her head and half raised a hand. Show over. The visitors went on to the ticket hut.

Matthew said despondently, 'I'm glad she had a happy weekend.'

'It will be a long time before she has another,' Dorothy said.

William said nothing. He went heavily through the flower-filled hall and out to the terrace. The plates of food were still there, the white chairs at angles, where they had been pushed back ten minutes ago. Leadenly, clumsily, he began to pile things on a tray. He felt bruised and sick, as if a mailed fist had come out of the sky and slammed him in the solar plexus.

All's well! All can never be well for more than the present moment. His excitement, his silly Sir Galahad dreams blown apart by Angela's face, her lovely face that he could never comfort and conjure to a smile again.

Gradually, they picked up the pursuits of the afternoon.

Dottie went to her desk to prepare her notes for a court appearance tomorrow. Forty Leckworth senior citizens had arrived in a purple coach, so Tessa went to help Ruth and Polly in the tea-room. As they were preparing to open, Ruth had got up the nerve to tell Doreen not to leave early, because she would like to speak to her after closing. That was what she meant to say. What came out was, 'Hang on a bit after. Don't go off, mind, and leave the sink like a cesspit.' Doreen had torn off the short white apron, thrown down a handful of spoons, breaking a saucer, and bicycled off the premises.

Nina went up to wash her hair. Matthew found a private place to read. William went out among the visitors to answer the same old questions and to chat to the knowledgeable in the slow, word-sparing language of gardeners. Might as well do something for someone.

He was wandering along the edge of the copse, looking for late cowslips, when the wiry man with the mad scientist hair and the silly green shoulder bag strode past him to the rougher grass farther up the hill. Probably a botanist or a horticulturist, he was here so often. He must spend a fortune in gate money, so William gave him a dutiful 'Afternoon'.

The man did not focus on William and did not answer. Off to do a bit of finger pruning, eh? Sneak cuttings? Dig up my white violets? 'What's in that bag?' Angela had asked, with that laugh in her voice, to make a mystery for Rob.

The curly white clouds spread and grew dingier as the day advanced and cooled. The late May heatwave, which had bewitched the weekend, was over. A pilot breeze sailed down the lake and blew the hair and see-through mac of a woman who was looking for carp among the lily pads. William was mooning about among the daylilies that should have been divided last year, but would have to wait, when Rob came running, head thrown back, eyes anguished, along the bank of the lake.

'Wum! Wum – you forgot!' He reached William, panting. 'I've been waiting and waiting.'

'What for?' William asked blankly.

'You *said*. I brought my sketches. You said about the drainage plan.'

'Oh, Rob.' William rubbed a hand over his face. 'I *am* sorry,' he started to say, but Rob cried, 'You forgot!' and ran towards the bridge, sobbing and dropping crumpled bits of paper. William picked them up and went after him.

Chapter Five

The following week, Ruth stayed with her grandmother while Agnes went shopping, a protracted affair that involved trawling the Oxford department stores with her friend Kath, having an argumentative lunch at Poppins and coming home cross, with the intention of taking back next week what she had bought.

Ruth spent most of the morning doing laundry and cleaning up the mess Agnes had accumulated in the kitchen and bathroom. After lunch, when Ruth had removed the soup and shreds of corned beef from the old lady's front and given her a chocolate cream, Mary Trout seemed quite bright and knowing.

Agnes was beginning to rave on a bit about nursing homes, but it was not time for that yet, and Ruth prayed it never would be. The Sanctuary was Mary Trout's life, almost all the life she had ever known, except for the first fourteen years with six people in half a dark, damp cottage at Goosey, toiling for her mother indoors and her father outside.

She knew today was Monday and the gardens were closed, and did not ask to have her chair moved nearer the side window to see the visitors coming up the drive. She asked about Doreen, because she was interested in everything that happened in the tea-room, or anywhere at The Sanctuary. Tessa always dropped in to gossip when she was here, and William came in almost every day with a bit of news to keep her going.

'Doreen?' Ruth was glad of the chance to talk about it. 'Took herself off at 1.30 yesterday, didn't she, on a busy Sunday, and I'm not going to trouble her to bring back the skirt and blouse, because I don't ever want to lay eyes on her again.'

'Oh, dear, you'll never manage. I'll come up and give you a hand.' Ruth's grandmother bit her bluish lips anxiously. 'Do you think Aggie will let me?'

Agnes was not such a tyrant, but Troutie, having lived under orders all her life, felt more comfortable if she still had a boss.

'That's all right, Gran,' Ruth said, 'I've had a wonderful stroke of luck. I put a little bit of an advertisement in the *Gazette*. Nobody answered, just like I thought. The people round here – I don't know what they want nowadays, but they don't want to work. I had to find somebody. I can't rely on Polly all the time, and Brenda won't touch teas. I was getting desperate.'

'Deshperate?' The faded old eyes searched Ruth's face.

'I didn't know what I was going to say to Will, he sets such store on everything being done right for the visitors.'

'Not like his mother,' the old lady half closed her crêpey eyelids, drifting into memory. 'Poor Miss Sylvia. Brought up as she was to society and entertaining, if guests came, she'd say, "Oh, damn, we're not putting on extra for them, Troutie. They can take us or leave us." But *her* mother, Lady Geraldine, she'd want to put the best of everything on the table, to impress.'

'Listen, Gran. I'm making egg and cress sandwiches, see, when suddenly along comes this woman like a bolt from the blue, like the angel Gabriel himself.' You had to ginger up your conversation to keep Gran listening. 'And it turns out she's living only a few miles away, and wanting part-time work.'

'She'll do?' The watery eyes, sparsely lashed, picked up the message from Ruth's eager face.

'She'll do, you're right. She's a good little worker, quick and neat, strong too, she can lift those boxes about, great with a jam sponge, and we've started shortbread again. I said *shortbread*, Gran. I'll fetch you some down if you'll wear your teeth. Nice enough looking, tackle anything, cheery with the customers. Pinch me, I must be dreaming. Good old Doreen. She walks out and Josephine walks in. Jo, I call her. A widow, poor soul, very sad. Her husband stopped eating and talking, went to choking, and was dead of cancer before he saw thirty-five. What do you think of that?'

But Mary Trout had drifted right away, shoulders hunched under the soft shawl Dorothy had brought her from Cotswold Weavers, hands like dead fish in the folds of her lap, head dropped on her sagging bosom, thin trail of saliva dribbling from one side of her empty mouth.

The May heatwave had broken in a lashing storm that rolled down from the hills to finish off the last of the spring blooms, and dash the hopes of some of the more delicate summer stock. A whole bed of orange Welsh poppies on the bank above the mausoleum was flattened. Late narcissi sprawled. The buds on William's new deutzia bushes were torn away from tender shoots. Two days of horizontal rain had put the marsh boardwalk under water, and John Dix ordered Keith out with Stuart and the trailer to pick up broken branches all over the grounds and pull down anything that might fall on a visitor.

'When we've had lunch,' Keith protested. He had a headache from the wind.

'Dinner can wait.'

'OK, OK.' Keith could not say that Dorothy was making him a toasted cheese sandwich at 12.30, because the understanding was that unless he was ill, he worked along with the others, and no favours.

When he came down the hill, kicked off his muddy boots and went up the back steps to the kitchen, Dottie had gone out and there was no cheese, nor anything to make a sandwich.

He went down to the tea-room with faint hope, because nobody would turn up for the gardens or the teas on such a foul day, but he found that a woman with dark hair and a wide expectant smile had the smaller urn simmering, flowers on the gingham cloths of each small table, and cakes laid out bravely.

'Hul-lo!' she said on a rising note, as if muddy Keith with plastered hair and splattered glasses were just the person she had hoped to see.

'Where's Ruth?' Keith was not supposed to cadge free hand-outs in the tea-room, but Ruth was always kind.

'I made her go home, with that cold. No sense in two of us waiting for no customers.'

'Where's Doreen?'

'She left. I'm Jo.' She wore a crisp white blouse over interest-ing breasts, and a flowered skirt, shorter than Ruth's, which revealed straight, vigorous legs.

'I'm Keith.'

'Can I get you tea?'

'I'm famished.'

She made him a pot of tea and a sandwich, and then another one.

Keith had no money in the pockets of his dungarees or his anorak.

'That's all right.' Jo folded strong bare arms under her high breasts. 'Work here, do you?'

'Yes, but . . .' Why was it difficult to say 'I'm one of the family'? Because her gaze through the thick dark lashes was so frank and approving that he did not want to see it diluted by caution.

'Never mind.' One set of lashes descended. 'I won't tell.'

'Thanks.' Keith picked up an eccles cake. 'Are you a temp then, or a fixture?'

'Oh, I'll stay.' She stood upright and passed a cloth over the counter. 'I like it here.'

'In spite of the – er – the noises?' Keith could not resist asking. He jerked his head towards the outer wall beyond which the foaling stable had burned down.

'What noises?' Jo kept the smile wide. She had a lot of good white teeth.

Keith told her.

'Oh,' she said, 'I don't pay any attention to that kind of thing.'

'*I* do.' He gave her the intense goggle that he practised in the mirror, along with other devices to add interest to his unremarkable face.

'Please yourself.'

William was in London most of the week. When Dorothy came home, Keith made chicken à la king and fried bananas.

At her clinic, Dorothy had seen a small boy, the only son of divorced parents: bed-wetting at six, night terrors, withdrawn at school – the classic loss–separation reactions.

'He made me think of Rob,' she told Keith. 'Hair in his eyes, long skinny legs, two big front teeth. Jittery, looking over his shoulder for trouble.'

'Father not interested?' Keith liked it when Doctor Dottie discussed cases with him.

'That's it, but the mother is obsessed. She makes him her whole life.'

'Poor little sod,' Keith said. 'At least you can't say that of Tessa.'

'She does dote on Rob, you know.'

'In her way.'

'Have more of this good rice, Keith. You're still horribly thin. Why didn't you come in for lunch?'

'I couldn't get away from the *führer*. I sneaked something later in the tea-room. Ruth wasn't there, but I conned the new woman.'

'That's not fair.' He couldn't con his aunt about rules.

'What do you think of her?' Keith changed the subject.

'All right so far.' Dorothy thought Jo was a real find, but she had seen too many come and go.

After Keith went to bed, she parcelled up the beautiful dressing-gown that Angela Stern had left behind in her distress. She knew that William had been enchanted, and that he had gone off to London depressed. Poor pet. Normal, though, at his age.

The following weekend Tessa had a conference at Hereford; on the Thursday her only reliable overnight baby-sitter cancelled. Too late to find anybody else. Rob could not stay at The Sanctuary, because his grandparents and Keith were going to a wedding. Ruth's cottage? Not fair, when Ruth had so much to do, even though she had apparently found a new body for the busy tea-room. Rob's other grandmother? That spoiled vindictive woman who had been heard to speculate, during the mess of Rex and Tessa's divorce, 'I've always thought Rob might not be his child anyway.' Never.

Rex? It was time he saw Rex anyway. After being with a father-and-son team like Rodney and Dennis, Rob began to say things like, 'Why does nobody bowl balls to me?'

'You want to play cricket, darling?'

'No.'

Tessa rang Rex at the office, so as not to risk talking to the new woman, sweet Rosalie.

'Rex. I won't keep you.' Tessa always said that quickly, before he could wound her with, 'Look, I'm really tied up just now.' 'Could you have Rob on Saturday and Sunday?'

'What? Wait . . . I don't see why not.'

'If we stay Friday night at The Sanctuary –'

'I can't pick him up there. I'm still taboo at the holy shrine.'

'I know that. I can bring him half way.' Rex, who was making a lot of money, lived with Rosalie in a pillared mansion near High Wycombe. 'Could you meet me at that hotel on the M40, The Crown, where we met before?'

'Our trysting place – ah, yes.' He put on a dreamy voice. 'Of course, Tess.' He switched on sincerity. 'I'll be glad to.'

It was still painful to hear the bastard's voice. Tessa hated and despised him now, but it still stabbed her to hear his voice. That voice. As irresistible as it had been when Tessa flung away everything for him in a blind consuming passion. No one had ever understood that it had been impossible to care, or even *think*, about his wife, 'poor Marigold'. Rex obliterated everything. There was nothing else.

No right or wrong. 'A sin?' her father had asked her once tentatively, when it came out that Marigold had tried to kill herself. 'Do you ever have black moments when you, er, when you think that what you have done might be a sin?'

'Nothing is a sin,' Tessa had told him then, presumptuously exalted, 'unless you think it is.'

It was less painful to see Rex in the flesh than to hear the intimate voice that carried such shivery memories. He was absurdly good-looking, better than ever at nearly forty, his mouth a snare for your eyes. But she knew what lay beneath all that. Beneath the superb white sweater and those jazzy joggers that bounced through a muzak-fouled hotel lobby where an ecstatic little boy rushed at him.

'Hey, old mate!' He bent to Rob, who put a puny stranglehold on his neck. When the child let him go, Rex stood up and looked at Tessa with those shameless grey eyes.

She had her organization-and-management-consultant clothes on, careful make-up, her caramel hair swept up and back in a sophisticated French pleat like a brandy snap.

'You look good.' Rex appraised her as if he still had the right to approve or not approve. 'Where are you off to?'

'Conference. Here's the hotel number, and Rob's things.' Her son was already on his way to the hotel door, holding his exercise book of drawings. 'I should get away late on Sunday afternoon, if you could bring him here.'

'Rosalie or I will.' (You come yourself, you bastard.) 'Call me when you know what time.'

They were two cool strangers, making efficient plans. He took the small purple backpack that said, 'Zermatt' and she turned away.

'My sessions start this afternoon. I've got to go,' she said.

'Recruitment in the Nineties' was a working conference for the personnel and training staff of a big London department store. Tessa had helped to design the programme with Dr Oscar Ferullo and the consultancy's psychologist. Oscar gave the main talks, and Tessa and the other assistants led small discussion groups.

Tessa enjoyed conferences. She liked staying in comfortable hotels. She liked knowing the language that everyone talked, and the small power of being a teacher.

By the end of a long Saturday afternoon, she was beginning to get the feel of some of this group's hidden conflicts, which Oscar would identify and work on tomorrow. 'Issues', they would be called – less threatening than 'problems'. In the career re-entry sessions she had to try to head off the tendency of each small group to degenerate into gossip or irrelevant personal grievances about married women and single mothers coming into the job market for training.

A woman with pink eyelids and a man with a coarse lower lip and jaw carried on interminably – 'I know it's true because my brother's wife –' seducing the rest into mistaking the particular for the general because they were tired, and it was better than working seriously. A man at the back with soft brown eyes and beard went quietly to sleep.

The real Tessa would have got up and told the group, 'I don't want to hear this rubbish,' and gone away to find a drink. Consultant Tessa, weary but still spruce, said, 'Do the rest of you really want to hear this?' The group took intelligent shape again and replied 'No'.

'You handled those morons pretty well.'

When Tessa was getting a drink at the bar for herself and Oscar, the man with the neat sweet beard was on a stool by her side.

'You were asleep.'

'Not with you in the room. Shall we get a bottle of wine and go into that other lounge where the good chairs are?'

'Just let me take Doctor Ferullo his drink.'

His name was Chris Harvey, and he was content to be in middle-level personnel, because he was also a potter, with a wheel and a kiln in his garage, and that was his real life. Having an unreliable car, he had come to Hereford by train, so at the end of the conference Tessa drove him back to Finchley. Because he was with her and she was on a high, Tessa rang Rex to say that she would pick Rob up at the mansion on her way into London.

Rosalie was indoors, or out, or drowned in the swimming pool. Tessa had never seen her. Rob was up a tree and Rex was fiddling with his big shiny ride-on mower, out on the front lawn, for effect. Chris stayed in the car, sorting through

Tessa's tapes with a view to recognizing her taste in music.

'How's he been?' Tessa asked Rex, leaning backwards to hold Rob, who had scrambled desperately into her arms, as if he had been rescued from purgatory.

'No problems.' Rex always said that, as he did if Tessa rang him to discuss a difficulty, implying: no problems with *me*.

'How has *he* been?' He looked towards Tessa's car.

'Exciting.' Tessa stuck out her tongue at him and put Rob down, and they galloped hand in hand across the drive, which was paved with square grey tiles, like a Mercedes advertisement. Chris leaned his head out of the car window with a charming smile for Rob. Tessa looked back, but Rex had his head down to the engine of the mower.

William had called in at the lodge cottage to see his darling old nurse Troutie, and to tell Agnes about the gutters.

'I'll get them seen to next week,' he said.

'My mother says she'll believe that when she sees it.'

Troutie was saying nothing, but Agnes used her as a ventriloquist's dummy for rude comments. 'She knows who's last on the list for repairs, and it's never the big house, is it?' If you caught her after lunch, with the morning hangover cleared and the foundation of tomorrow's laid, Agnes did not care what she said to anyone.

Having delivered his message about the gutters, William wanted to go, but he worried about Agnes's drinking, and so he nerved himself to say something.

'Not happy here?' he began.

'I do as well as can be expected, Mr Taylor.' Her mother called him by his childhood name, Billie, and Ruth had always known him as Will, but Agnes stuck to Mr Taylor in public and private, because she felt that people like him should be kept in their place.

'And I'm sure we're all grateful.'

Agnes narrowed her eyes at him over her cigarette. What was he up to? 'It's no more than my duty.'

'Yes, but – well, don't take this the wrong way, Agnes, but there is a bit of a problem, isn't there?'

'Old people are always a problem.' Agnes jerked her bulldog chin towards her mother, who was silent, lids lowered, but listening.

'I mean – we all know you have a bit of a problem with alcohol.' He had learned that from Dottie, a modish way of saying, 'You're a lush.'

'*All?* Who's *all?*'

'Well – the family.'

'The family.' Agnes made a face as if she saw dog mess on the carpet. 'What business is it of theirs? Hasn't *my* family given enough of their lives to *your* family?'

'Well, of course . . . But look, we could get a companion for your mother.'

'Cost the earth.'

'We'd pay, of course.'

'No one's ever paid *me*.'

'Is that what you want?'

'Mr Taylor.' Agnes tossed her head of faded thinning hair that had been permed to the consistency of breakfast cereal. 'This is my mother.'

When Agnes had gone out of the room, Troutie opened her eyes.

'Don't worry about me, Billie.' She croaked, as she always did after silence. 'It's you I'm worried about.' She cleared her throat harshly, but the fluid was deeper, down in her lungs. 'You don't look quite yourself, my dear.'

'I'm not.' Because the anxiety was still with him, and the pain, he told Troutie about the Sterns' weekend, and the appalling tragedy of Angela's son's death. He turned away as he told it, and looked out of the window at a flock of bicyclists in tight shiny shorts, because his eyes had begun to water and his voice was unsteady.

'Dead.' Troutie's lungs laboured, wheezing. 'Ah, dear. Lose a son . . . never get over it. Your grandmother never did.'

Dead. Just that word, like a stone dropped, after Sir Frederick has read the telegram. Dead. It passes through the house, up to Miss Sylvia in the schoolroom, and down, from lip to lip, past young Mary on her knees with the wax polish, through the pantry and the servants' hall and the kitchen and sculleries and all the endless cold passages. Dead.

'He died like a hero, Mr Lionel, leading his men over the top. It was as if all the lights went out at The Sanctuary.'

'What was he – twenty? And my poor mother . . .'

'Miss Sylvia was only thirteen, and young with it. At fourteen, I was years older in my ways. I saw what happened. I saw it, Billie. Lady Geraldine – it was like she had to punish Sylvia for being alive.'

William knew his mother's sad little story: how this plain shy girl had been oppressed, and forbidden to marry a man who was 'unsuitable'.

'I was the only one she could talk to. "Go with him," I said. "Leave all for love."'

'Why didn't she?' William's memories of his mother were clouded with a thousand failures.

'Because he got fed up of being scorned by the family, and went away to Scotland.'

Troutie went into a coughing fit. She came out of it gasping, and said weakly, 'I loved your mother.'

'I never understood her.'

'No good with children. That's why I took over.'

'Thank God you did.'

The old lady's head dropped forward and her purple lids

came down, hollowly, as if there were no eyeballs behind. William went out, and as he passed her window he looked in at the crouched heap of stuffy clothes and moulting hair. Even as she slept, the heap jerked convulsively, and she was racked with that appalling cough that sounded as if her lungs were flooded with boiling filthy water.

Coughing like that in June! Next winter would be worse for her than last. She'd drown in it. Better to die now, William thought bitterly. Why struggle on to reach ninety, when Angela's Peter, a young man of eighteen, could be obliterated in an inferno of screaming metal?

'Like it here?' William asked the new woman in the tea-room. He had stopped in to ask Ruth about getting the doctor back for her grandmother's cough. No good asking Agnes, who mistrusted doctors.

'*Very* much.'

Jo was scooting about with a tray, clearing tables speedily. Like Ruth, she went on working while she talked. Poor young woman, not long widowed. Cancer, what a tragedy. Should I say something about her husband? Not much good at things like that. Would I have known what to say to Angela if she had been at home when I rang her yesterday?

'I'm fascinated by this old place and its history,' Jo said, wiping a slopped table efficiently, cupping the mess into a cloth, the way women do.

'Ask Ruth to take you to see her grandmother,' William said. 'She remembers everything about the old days.'

'Could I?' Jo asked Ruth. 'I'd love that.' She had an enthusiastic, slightly stagey voice, as if she might once have been, or tried to be, an actress. Her dark fringe was cut narrow, with the straight black hair close to her face, curving up to points at her chin.

'Of course, my dear.' Ruth seemed to like her. William

would probably like her when he got to know her. He was depressed now, and not interested.

As Ralph's party had left the restaurant after the Barrett Mayne dinner, William had asked him, 'How is – how is Angela?'

'Shattered,' Ralph said too easily, his host's urbanity still operating. 'She's gone to her sister's for a bit. Totally to pieces.'

Angela . . . my dazzling brief companion. You spun in and out of my life and showed me a vision. Now I can't help you. Why should you need me?

He did not try to ring Angela again.

It was the most exciting thing that had ever happened in Frank's ornithological life. He had suspected that the wilder reaches of The Sanctuary estate might yield good rewards. But even he, a dreamer, a visionary, had never hoped for a prize like this.

The Friday after he and Faye had been at The Sanctuary and he had helped that funny little boy ('Strange how you're always so ready to butt into the lives of total strangers,' Faye had said when he caught up with her in the car park), he had dropped her off at her afternoon job at the cottage hospital and gone back to the fabulous gardens. He paid his two pounds at the white wooden kiosk, scooted up the hill and crouched among the overgrown vegetation on the far side of the coppice. He saw a chiff-chaff and heard a willow-warbler's liquid descending song; a pair of wrens were pecking about under some bushes as if they were looking for last year's berries. And then he saw it – a long patch of off-white underparts – only for a moment, so at first he thought he might be mistaken. The little bird flitted back at once among the branches. When he saw the broad chestnut tail, his heart stopped in its tracks and then raced, and he had to swallow to cope with the rush of emotion that filled his throat.

A nightingale. Once the poets' familiar, now among the rarest of birds. Gone, long gone, Juliet's nightingale – 'Nightly she sings on yon pomegranate tree' – because modern farming had destroyed most of the thickets and hedgerows. Last year, there were said to be no more than half a dozen pairs in Oxfordshire.

But here was one, and it was his alone.

Because he had to get to the shops before they closed, Frank had crept quietly away so as not to alarm this shyest of birds. He had pranced down the hill with a great grin on his bony mug. By the lake, little groups of visitors were walking, pointing things out to each other, stooping to peer at a label, sitting contentedly on a rustic bench to take in the whole satisfying English scene, with the strong stone house four-square in its idyllic setting.

Two men with a barrow and an assortment of dogs were thinning out iris corms on a bank by the water. The taller one was lanky in old trousers and open blue shirt, the other balder, shorter, stockier, in clothes too clean and towny to be messing about with clumps of wet iris. They did not look like gardeners.

'Excuse me,' Frank said when he came across a real gardener raking out a shrubbery bed. 'May I ask who that might be?'

The gardener straightened up and looked. 'That's Mr Taylor, Mr William Taylor, that is, who lives here, and that other, that's his brother, Matthew Taylor.'

The next day, after Frank had been up to look for the nightingale again, he saw the lanky one in a dinghy on the lake with the little lost boy and a smashing woman, so he could say jauntily, 'Afternoon, Mr Taylor. Lovely day for a sail,' and swing over the narrow hump-backed bridge as if he were a privileged customer.

Which he was – oh, he was! Little did they know, those three people in the boat, laughing about nothing and looking up a little surprised when he greeted them so familiarly from the bridge, that he, Frank Pargeter, had been in the undergrowth up there with his binoculars trained on not one but a pair of little brown nightingales darting in and out among the nettles and brambles with leaves and grass in their tiny sharp beaks, and shreds of sheep's wool to line their home.

No one must know. They must not even know he was a bird man. His Leitz binoculars were concealed in the green shoulder bag one of the children had used to take sandwiches to school centuries ago. He could tell no one, not even Roger, his trusted friend, because ornithologists could not always keep a secret, and if the news leaked out, all the twitchers would come to tick it off on their Must list, and you couldn't be safe from the egg thieves – that gang from Southampton who would flog them illegally, or try raising the chicks to sell to sleazy exhibitions in unpleasant pleasure parks.

He certainly would not tell Faye, who wouldn't care anyway. She didn't mind him birdwatching as long as she didn't want the car. Indeed she was glad to have him out of the house, since the thought of him leaving tea bags in the sink and laying out his photographs on the dining-room table was just as irritating to her whether she was at home or not. But she understood nothing of the subtleties of the hobby, and might, with or without malice, let loose a story to one of her cynical pals, entitled, 'Frank's Obsession'.

The Sanctuary was only twenty minutes away from Frank's scrupulous red-brick house, with a sodium street lamp that glared into the front bedrooms, where he and Faye had brought up their children in fear of the main road, before the motorway rose behind them to deafen them with safety.

Faye was often busy – bending down four-square from her elephant's rump in the garden, into which beer bottles and hamburger containers sailed from time to time, or doing afternoons on the hospital switchboard, where she gave the third degree to enquirers from behind the desk in the highly polished entrance hall, a skating rink for dithery old ladies. So Frank was able to come to The Sanctuary often. Sometimes he saw the nightingales, sometimes he didn't. It was getting too expensive to come in by the visitors' entrance, but reconnoitring farther up the hill, he had found a gap in the crumbling boundary wall and a farm track where he could leave the car hidden behind a disused storage shed.

Under pretence of going to a meeting of his local branch of the Royal Society for the Protection of Birds, he was even able to sneak in here one night, his heart on tiptoe, and lie silently on a bed of bracken to hear the bubbling clicks of the 'Chook-chook-chook' rise to the intoxicating crescendo, 'Piu, piu, piu,' as if the bird would never stop. One down for you, Faye, with your church choir and your all-girl hand-bells. Only the male can do this.

One afternoon Frank scrambled over the wall to discover the best treat of all – the male bird with half a worm in its beak, nipping across the open space between two bushes as if there were a sniper in the trees. So the old lady was on her eggs. It was all going according to nature's plan, and Frank's summer was made. Because his hiding place must be twenty or thirty yards away, he would never set eyes on the nest itself. But she was sitting, that was sure. The old man would not be out doing the shopping unless she was employed. You and me both, mate.

It was a bit chilly today and raining on and off, so he stole out of his hide. Too early to collect Faye. He would drop down the hill, heel and toe with elbows going to warm up, and have a reviving cup of tea in Mr William Taylor's delightful tea-room.

He knew the nice comfortable woman with soft brown hair and amber glasses, but not this younger, quicker one with black hair and a dark Mediterranean glance who filled his teapot from the urn.

'Where's Ruth today?' he asked.

'Taken a bit of time off, as the weather's made this a slow day. I'm in charge, ha ha.'

Frank put the teapot, milk, a cup and two cakes on his tray and carried it to a table near the counter. There were only a few tables filled. The woman was not busy. When she brought him hot water, she said, 'Not your first visit here, then?'

'Oh, no, I come fairly often.'

'I don't blame you. It's gorgeous, isn't it, the flowers and trees and the whole . . . the whole . . .' She sketched the beauties of The Sanctuary with generous gestures of her arms and hands.

'Oh, yes, I agree.' He liked her wide smile and the high pointy breasts under the immaculate white shirt, about two feet higher than where Faye's were now.

'And the birds.' She put her head on one side. 'Even though there's cats about, and I gather there always have been, with a temple raised in their honour, there is birdsong everywhere in the blossoming trees.'

'Nesting time,' Frank said. 'The males warning interlopers off their territory.'

'I don't care if it's a male macho thing.' She gave him a wag of the head, as if he might be guilty of that himself. 'It's sweet to your ears, just as the garden fills your eyes.'

'Are you a bird person then?' Frank asked. The RSPB ought to have a secret finger sign, like the Masons.

'Oh, yes, I am.'

A lesser man might have been tempted to tell her the great secret. Her warm red mouth would stretch even farther sideways, and her dark eyes would be entranced. But with Frank, it was safe. When he paid she said, 'See you again, perhaps?' and he replied glibly, 'Doubtless. I'm studying deciduous trees at the agricultural college, doing a thesis on some of the more exotic variations that have been able to thrive in this part of the country.'

He had worked that up to explain his frequent presence here, if necessary. It was useful to be able to try it out.

Coming to work one day on her bicycle, Jo was passed by a sporty red car with a woman driver, and a small boy in the back seat. The car put on its indicator, slowed, then turned under the wrought iron arch between the stone pillars of The Sanctuary. A small woolly dog was standing on the shelf inside the back window, wagging its tail.

Too early for garden visitors. Must be someone for the house. As Jo rode slowly down the drive between the candelabras of the chestnut trees, she saw the car circle the gravel space and stop by the front door.

At the turn-off to the stableyard Jo dismounted, wheeled her bicycle to the rearing pony statue and leaned it against the base. Then she stepped quickly along the wall that separated the front of the house from the back entrances and outbuildings. A niche at the end of the wall held an urn of dark pink geraniums. If anyone saw her, she was picking out dead flowers, devoted servant of The Sanctuary that she was.

A young woman with shoulder-length, bright brown hair, wearing a short white skirt and orange top, was reaching into the car for bags. The dog jumped out and ran up the steps and barked. The little boy got out and started after it. The woman called to him, holding out a small bag, but he went on up the steps and put his puny weight against one of the great double doors of the fortress and went inside. The woman threw the soft bag up to the top of the steps, shut the door of the car and turned to follow him. Round the open front door came the head and shoulders of William Taylor. The bright-haired woman looked up with a radiant smile of greeting.

Tessa Taylor! The old vile pain of hatred surged up from deep within to flood Jo's battered heart and pound in her brain so dizzyingly that she had to lean against the flower urn for support.

Jo had seen Tessa's picture once in a magazine, with Rex at a party, half naked at the top, silky black trousers clinging to every curve and crevice. As Mr Taylor came down to take her bag, she kissed him on or near the mouth, and bounced up the steps and through the door, her bottom wagging the pleated skirt from side to side.

Dirty tramp. Now that the first agonizing moment was past, now that Jo had seen her at last, the turmoil was calmed and the steep breathless rise in her expectation of waiting was halted. Plenty of time now. Now was when it all began.

She turned away from the geranium urn and wheeled her bicycle across the courtyard, head up, the thick rubber soles of her white working shoes springing on the cobbles.

She did not see tarty Miss Tessa any more that day. Ruth talked about her and the boy Rob while they were getting the teas ready, as she relayed to Jo any news of family or friends coming and going, like a daily newspaper. When Jo went up to get the last batch of baking out of the oven, she saw the child with his grandmother in the kitchen – *Rex's child*.

'Hullo, Jo,' Dorothy Taylor said. 'Something smells good.'

'Bath buns.' Jo bent to lift the old dark trays out of the Aga.

'Look, Rob, here's a new friend.' The boy's grandmother pulled him gently from behind her, where he had taken refuge from this stranger. 'This is Mrs Kennedy, who's working with Ruth in the tea-room.'

'Oh, he can call me Jo, like everyone else. Would you like a hot bun, Rob?'

He nodded, and she put a Bath bun on the table, where he and Dorothy were making a salad. He was a thin child, long-legged in short shorts, forelock of dark hair hiding his cautious eyes. Not his father's eyes. Not that look of bold, world-conquering amusement. But the perfectly drawn wing of eyebrow had been passed on, giving his small face an unchildlike definition.

That evening in her small cottage two miles away, Jo went upstairs to review herself in the mirror behind the cupboard door.

Perfect. In the unlikely event that any of these people or their friends had ever seen her before, they would not recognize her. Even Rex might not know her, if he came here, which she had gathered from Ruth he never did.

'Right, Marigold,' she said to her reflection, then dropped the Jo-speak that came so chummily through the stretched smile, and let her face and voice fall back to her own quiet, unstressed style. 'You're all right.' Jo's eyes looked back at Marigold through the dark tinted contact lenses that she had told the optician were needed for a film part. If her eyes had been born coal black like a Hardy heroine, instead of that washed-out sandy green, her life might have been different.

She took off the pretty bucolic uniform and threw it down the stairs to wash. If the fine weather held, tomorrow would be a busy last Saturday in June, and she must always be good Jo, spotless and perfect, the tea-room treasure. She removed the firmly padded bra, pulled a cotton sweatshirt over her modest breasts, and took off her bracelets and the large white and gold ear-rings: daisies, to match the flowered skirt. Marigold had usually worn small gold or pearl studs, but the whole costume jewellery department could be a playground for Josephine.

Downstairs, she poured a glass of wine, and went out into

the tangled garden between her cottage and the Richardsons'
patchy 1920s bungalow, where they cooked fish and bred
Siamese cats. Most evenings she hacked away at the jungle
with a sickle Mr Richardson had lent her. Gradually the
sodden ruins of a grass plot were emerging from the undergrowth that slothful tenants had allowed to lay siege to Bramble
Bank. Soon she would borrow a mower and cut the chickweed
and plantains and mosses down to something that resembled a
lawn, in case any of the Taylors demeaned themselves enough
to pay a call on good old Jo.

'Do come to tea, Miss Tessa, and bring the dear little lad.
We couldn't get glacé cherries, so we're serving deadly night-
shade in the sultana loaf.'

'Good evening, Josephine.' Mr Richardson was out in his
hillocky potato patch beyond the rusted iron fence that Jo was
going to replace with white wooden rails. 'The arthritis is
terrible.' He never waited for you to ask.

'Oh, dear. Shall I come and hoe for you?' She was not just a
saint at The Sanctuary. Her reputation must spread far and
wide.

'You've got enough to do, my dear. I wish I could help *you*.'

'You're a pal,' said Jo.

Sod off, thought Marigold. I don't need help from anybody.
In the house, she drank half the glass of wine and muttered
back and forth between her kitchen and living-room. Shut up,
Marigold, don't crowd back in. Think Jo. Josephine. Poor,
brave Josephine. Think widow. She took up the photograph of
an unknown young man with curly hair and an inoffensive
moustache and glared at it, holding it in both hands. Then, as
the unseen director of her days commanded, 'Roll 'em,' she
melted into her wide Jo smile and shook her head tenderly
and pressed the photograph to her shallow bosom. 'Alec –
dearest . . .'

Chapter Six

Because Tessa and her child were there, Jo spent some time up at the big house, keeping her eyes and ears open, noting things that might come in useful, establishing herself as part of The Sanctuary.

She came up in the morning and explored more of the gardens, which she was allowed to do, as a member of the staff. She had only seen the weird old mausoleum from the other side of the lake, so she crossed the bridge and found the overgrown steps that led from the top of the mound down to the tomb's entrance.

Clutching the full flowered skirt round her legs (Marigold would gladly have set fire to it, but Jo was conscientious about the uniform), she scrambled down through the ivy and junipers. As she stood on the wide marble slab between the tomb and the water examining the inscription and the spread wings on the doors, she saw a small absorbed figure in swimming trunks wading about in the shallow water farther down the lake.

She climbed up the steps and went along the bank to where Rob was messing about with a funnel and some pieces of pipe.

'Hullo again. I'm Jo, remember?' Although he was a painful reminder of what Tessa had had with Rex and she had not, Jo was going to try to get close to the child, to get him on her side.

'I saw you at the mouse-o-leum,' he said, head down, scrabbling for something in the mud. He was shy but friendly enough, like most only children who spend a lot of their time with grown-ups. 'There's bodies in there, you know.'

'Oh, I don't think so,' Jo said. 'One of the gardeners told me that they were taken away long ago to lie in the churchyard.'

Rob lost interest. 'I'm good at plumbing,' he said. 'Me and my grandfather are going to drain a bit of this marsh, so we can build a bandstand.'

'That sounds exciting.'

'The silver band can play here, if we get it done in time for the Festival. I'm going to let off rockets.'

'When is that?'

'End of August.'

'You'll have to get on with it, then.'

'Oh, we will. Me and my grandfather have drawn the master plan.'

'Will you be a plumber when you grow up?'

Jo was afraid she was being too arch, but Rob said, 'Of course. And the first thing I'll do is tear out that Flusher.' He stood upright and pushed back his wet hair. His large rectangular front teeth clamped on his bottom lip. His face had changed from workmanlike satisfaction to a sort of fearful determination.

'What's Flusher?'

He told her. 'It eats babies. Come in the house. I'll show you. The cellars too.'

He waded out on to the bank and took her hand. He likes me. Well done, old Jo. Would he like Marigold?

She had not been into the great house yet, except up the back stairs and into the baking pantry where she and Ruth made up their doughs and cake mixes, and into the kitchen, to use the Aga.

She must not take liberties; she had to tell the child, 'I've got to start getting things together for this afternoon.'

She helped Rob to carry his pipes and bottles to the back of the house. He dropped them where someone would fall over them, and disappeared.

Keith was in the kitchen, slicing vegetables to make cold soup. He heard someone come up the short stairs from outside and go into the back pantry. 'Ruth?'

'It's me,' Jo called out in her clear sing-song. She seemed to be coming in earlier and earlier. Doreen had always skulked in late, but Jo turned up before Ruth most days, and started bashing pans and rolling-pins about. 'How are you, on this lovely day?'

She was always so damn cheerful. Worse than Ruth. Bit depressing, if you were having a low day.

'Depressed.'

'I'm sorry.' Jo came to the doorway between the two rooms. 'That's a result of your illness, isn't it? My cousin's daughter had it.'

'Did she?' Keith was pleased. Nobody ever seemed to know anything about ME. 'Hit her hard?'

'Oh, terrible. All sorts of problems. We thought she might go blind, at one point.'

'I had double vision for a week. My mother thought I'd been drinking.'

Jo went back to her bowls and boards, and they talked back and forth comfortably, two people working.

'Rob wanted to take me through the cellars,' Jo said.

'He's morbid. Did he tell you about the ghost of Maryann Button who hung herself in the game room?'

'Hung herself?' Jo brought a broad smile into the doorway, dangling doughy hands. 'Goodness, how spooky. He's already told me about a toilet that eats babies.'

'Rob likes to alarm himself, but it's all fantasy. This isn't a spooky place.'

70

'I don't believe in psychic phenomena anyway. Do you?'

Because she glibly dismissed all the supernatural possibilities of the universe and took her sticky hands so cheerfully back to her work, Keith was moved to say gloomily, 'I live at The Sanctuary. Anything is possible.'

'Like what?'

'I prefer not to talk about it.'

Jo came in early on Sunday as well, because Ruth liked to go to church with her family. As she was sweeping the porch and the cobbles outside the tea-room, Dorothy Taylor rode into the stableyard on the large grey pony.

'You're in early,' she called to Jo.

Jo leaned on her broom in the time-honoured posture of maidservants. 'A lot to be done, Mrs Taylor.' Then, in case that could be interpreted as a veiled complaint, she added, 'I like to get ahead of the day. You're *out* early, for that matter.'

'Same reason. I've got work to do, and people coming to lunch *and* dinner.'

She led the pony under the clocktower arch to the other part of the yard where the loose boxes were. Jo left her broom and followed her. The pony stopped by its own stable and put its head over the door while Dorothy unbuckled the girth.

'You always seem so busy,' Jo said. 'Perhaps you'd like me to help you in the house sometimes.'

'Oh, *no*, you're needed in the tea-room.'

'I could come in at other times. My time's my own now.'

Dorothy Taylor was too shrewd to be conned into harmonizing 'Yes, poor you' to the 'poor widow' tune, as some people did. She said briskly, 'That's all right. I've got Mrs Smallbone. And Ruth and Brenda give me a hand if I need them.' She put the saddle on the half door and took the pony inside.

Not the first time you've brushed me off, Dorothy, if you

only knew it. You brushed off poor Marigold when I came here looking for your help: 'I must ask you to leave' – oh, that cool, secure voice.

But Jo was a different customer. Any way she could, she would get into the house, infiltrate this confident family and destroy it from within, like a weevil.

'Don't forget,' she said over the stable door. 'If you ever do need extra help . . .'

'Get over,' Dorothy said to the pony.

There was a mirror in the tea-room scullery, because Ruth was inclined to get flushed and dishevelled on a hot busy day. Jo looked in it to confirm once again that neither Dorothy nor William could connect their long-ago glimpse of rain-sodden Marigold with this sunny, obliging person with the bright, noticeable mouth. Good thing red lipstick was in again now, for her new smile. Very different from the unassuming mouth that had attracted no attention in the days of the pale cantaloupe lipstick.

The drastic hair colouring and the eyebrow and eyelash dye were holding up well. Her lashes had not looked nearly as thick as this when they were sandy. Now that she had got used to it, she liked herself as a dark lady. How had she ever put up with being colourless? *Because Rex had liked it.* The first time they met, he had said, 'You make every other woman in the room look like a cartoon.'

In those early undeveloped days when he fancied he was artistic, he had adored Marigold's opaque ivory skin. He had wanted her not to use make up, to let her pallid hair grow and arrange it very simply, to wear flat heels, so that the contrast between his height and hers was even more dramatic. When they were with noisy people, he wanted her to be the quiet one, for effect. 'The still calm centre of that hellish throng,' he said at home later, pleased with her, turning her into an inferno in bed.

Jo busied herself checking the stores, making a list for Ruth's orders tomorrow. She stood on the step stool to get the big cake tins down. She weeded out broken biscuits and tired rock cakes into a bowl of crumbs that would be scattered for the fantails. Customers liked to see the symbolic white birds pecking about.

She could imagine Rex here as a son-in-law, slumming it in the tea-room – what a riot – among all the old ducks and daddies, mooching casually round the corner, hands in pockets, eyes crinkled against the western sun, expecting instant attention from Ruth, as he had long ago from Marigold when she was busy.

That was when Rex still needed her, not just the money with which she could fuel his ambitions. But after he met Tessa – no, long before that, when he was dabbling with women about whom Marigold pretended to know nothing, because she still believed that fable that if you were patient, they would come back to you – the very things that had intrigued Rex about Marigold gradually became grievances.

Ruth bustled in with her wicker trays of fruit cake. 'Better check the stores first thing, so I can get my list done for the Cash and Carry.'

'I've done it.'

'Oh, you are a marvel, Josephine. Thanks ever so. We're in good time, then.'

'I made tea when I saw your car. You can sit for a minute.'

Ruth beamed. They sat at one of the tables, colleagues, good friends. Ruth admired the charm bracelet which Jo had put together to embellish the saga of Alec.

'This heart was for our fifth anniversary. The fish we bought in Cornwall when we were doing the cliff walk. The little bell . . . Alec said he liked to know where I was. And he got me the silver book because we used to read the same books, you see, and talk about them.'

'Miss him, don't you?' Ruth's comfortable face was so kind.

Jo nodded, then pushed back her hair and said courageously, 'Back to work.'

'We could do with some more flowers.' Ruth stood up. 'I'll start on the sandwiches, if you'll run up to the cutting garden and get us a big bunch.'

'Will anyone mind?'

'They'd better not. We help to support this place, and I'm not waiting for those gardeners to bring down what bits of rubbish they might condescend to spare us.'

Returning from the walled plot where vegetables and flowers were grown for the house, Jo saw William Taylor and his daughter coming across the lawn, and although she was glad to be seen looking picturesque with an armful of flowers, she made a detour to avoid Tessa. She had not yet seen her close to, or spoken to her. She was not quite ready. It could wait. Ruth had told her that Tessa came here often.

'She loves it in the summer, and she needs to be with her family, poor dear, having gone through so much.'

Excuse me while I vomit.

'"Upsets me," I said to George, "to see her so thin." Quite haggard she was for a while.'

'What did George say?'

'Nothing.'

If you'd said it to me, I could have told you. Save your sympathy. She got what she wanted. Stole a man and then dropped him when it suited her. Haggard? She didn't give a damn.

'Who's that?' Tessa asked, as the woman with flowers turned on to the path behind the rhododendrons.

'The new helper in the tea-room. Great success. I take my hat off to her, coping so well after such a recent tragedy.' He explained Jo's situation.

'It must be horrible.' Tessa looked inwards, as women do when they hear of a new widow. 'Wum, dear.' She put an arm through his.

'What do you want?'

'Nothing. Just to tell you a secret.'

She had come here determined not to say anything about Chris, because families could wither a budding affair on the vine quicker than a late frost. But her father was confidable.

'Tell me.' He inclined his head towards her.

'*Well*. I've got a – at least, I think I've got – a new man.'

'Is that the fellow on the phone too late last night and too early this morning?'

'No, that was Colin. You know Colin. The one with the jokes.'

William groaned.

'This is . . .' Suddenly she was shy about saying Christopher's name, because it meant so much, and brought an instant image of his gentle presence that somehow smelled of hay, even in Finchley. 'His name is Chris Harvey and he's lovely. Mid-thirties, and he's a potter and a sort of sculptor too.' She did not mention the department store.

'So Colin is out of luck?'

'Not really. I'm not cutting everybody else off. No commitment. I've had that. Never again.'

'Till the next time. Why don't you bring the sculptor down here? He can inspect the statuary.'

'That's the thing . . . I'd like to. Can I bring him some weekend? I'd love you to meet him.'

Before she left The Sanctuary, Tessa went to the tea-room, where Ruth and the new woman Jo were taking chairs down off tables.

'Hullo. I'm Tessa Taylor.' She had gone back proudly to her own name after the divorce, although that stupid Marigold was still sagging about calling herself Mrs Renshaw. Rob was still legally Robert William Renshaw, but Tessa called him Robert Taylor.

Jo smiled very warmly and put out a hand. Got to touch this Tessa some time. May as well start now.

'I just wanted to say hullo and goodbye before I go back to London. I – I wanted to say I'm glad you're here, and I'm sorry about your husband. It's – so awful.'

She was embarrassed – good – eyes darting a bit.

'How did he die?'

Jo told her the oft-rehearsed story that was beginning to take on a reality of its own.

'So young . . . What was he like?'

Jo went to her bag and took a small snapshot out of her wallet. Not the same man as the one framed in the cottage, but near enough.

'This was him when he was starting to be ill.'

'Yes, he is quite thin. He looks so nice.' Tessa looked up at Jo, creasing her brow with genuine pity.

'He was.' The brave little widow could say it with only a tiny tremor of the lip.

Chapter Seven

Now that Jo had seen Tessa and talked to her, she wanted desperately to know more. She must know everything about her. It was almost like being in love.

One Monday when the gardens and tea-room were closed, she drove up to London and scouted round the tidy little streets of Acton, sizing up the neighbourhood, noting the tube station and the wine shop and the post office which Tessa probably used, before she parked the car and walked towards the street where she knew Tessa and Rob lived. Jo had bundled her dark hair into a scarf, and left off the jewellery and bright assertive make-up. She wore a dreary raincoat from the old days, and dark glasses and flat shoes.

Viewed from behind a large car across the street, 47 Brackett Road had attractive arches over the windows in a lighter brick than the rest of the house and its attached neighbour. The front door was yellow, the window frames and gutters white, all the paintwork sparkling. A small paved front garden had tubs of riotous plants Miss Tessa had probably nicked from her father's nursery beds.

No signs of life, so Jo went back to her car and drove through Shepherd's Bush to Holland Park and along one of the streets that curved round Lansdowne Hill to the pink corner house which had been her hell after she lost Rex. The square, well-balanced house looked innocent and hopeful. The windowsills were full of plants. There was a toy pedal car outside the garage. When Jo stopped the car, the sound of children's voices from the fenced garden cut her in two, and she had to bend over the steering wheel, gasping for breath. How *could* they? How could a family be living cheerfully in this house as if nothing had gone wrong here? What had happened to all the pain? Where was the ghost of the nameless unformed being whose bloody death should shame into silence the laughter of children here for ever?

Go home, Marigold. Go back to Jo's home in the country, where she has shoved the pain into the background, to be out of the way of the driving purpose.

But going west down Holland Park Avenue in the clotted traffic, she found she did not want to turn towards the motorway. She had to go straight on through Shepherd's Bush and find her way back to Tessa's street on the chance of seeing her returning from somewhere, coming home from this famous work of hers which Ruth rattled on about, but could not exactly explain.

Jo walked up the opposite side of Tessa's road again, moving slowly behind the parked cars. She crossed and recrossed the top end of the street, looking down the slope of Brackett Road. She turned down it again and stepped behind a van as she saw her quarry, the jaunty red car backing into a space. Tessa sat in it with a man. They were laughing. He put a hand across her shoulders. She leaned her head towards him, a smaller head, with the loose shining hair pulled up neatly into a chic urban coil.

They sat there outside the house, liking each other, too busy with this present moment to get out and start the next one.

One morning when Marigold and Rex were living in that pretentious development house with the kitchen window at the front, they were washing up last night's dinner-party dishes quite amicably. Rex was dressed. Marigold was still in her nightgown, because the more uneasy she was about Rex, the harder it was to get up. This morning, she felt more hopeful. Perhaps the old lore was right. Give them some rein, and they will come back.

Rex quite suddenly put down the dish towel and went out of the room. Thinking he had gone up to the bathroom, Marigold finished the drying, went upstairs with her coffee mug, and took off her nightdress.

'Rex?' He wasn't there. He wasn't in the house. She looked out of the front bedroom window and saw him sitting in a car with a woman in it, shamelessly parked at the end of the short drive.

Rex got out of the car and came up the drive, smirking. As he opened the door and came into the hall, an enraged woman, a virago stark naked on the stairs, threw hot coffee all over him, mug and all.

The relief had been wonderful, for a very short time. As soon as she had stopped screaming, Marigold was horrified at herself. Rex never talked about it, and nor did she. There was already no point.

Now, as the door of Tessa's car opened, Jo turned and walked away. From the corner of her eye, she saw Tessa and a nondescript man with a soft beard cross the pavement, open the glossy gate and go up the short steps into the house. In a minute or two, a fat young baby-sitter with unbrushed hair came out and walked down the road towards the station.

On a Friday in mid July, William came back from Somerset and told Dottie that the equestrian centre deal was going through. Ralph Stern's enigmatic friends were putting up a substantial amount of money, with Ralph himself somehow involved.

Yesterday when he had to ring Ralph at home early in the morning before the final meeting, Angela had answered the telephone.

'He's in Newcastle.' She had given him the number of the hotel, and then said, 'Will, don't hang up. Let's talk.'

'I've wanted to. I couldn't reach you. Angela, I – I don't know what to say.'

'You don't need to. One of the worst agonies is watching people struggling to say the right thing about Peter.' She still had a little laugh in her voice, but no joy in it, only strain.

William said, 'How are you?'

'Terrible.'

'I'm sorry.'

'I know.'

They waited. It was Angela who said, 'Can we meet again? I think I need to talk to you.'

'I'd like that. Shall I –?'

'Wait,' she said. 'I'll see.'

They could have met quite openly to talk as friends, but she had ended on a paused, secret note that filled him with a flushed emotion he could not identify at first, but which he later recognized as fear. Telling Dottie about the Somerset negotiations, he was gentle and loving with her, to exorcize his unease.

'Will you mind if I play in the Shiplock match tomorrow?' He sometimes played cricket for the village team. 'They want Matthew to play too.'

'That should terrify Shiplock. Why should I mind?'

'It's going to be a busy weekend, with all the family. You'll have a lot to do.'

'Tessa will help. Don't worry, Will. What's the matter?'

'Nothing. All's well. I'm a lucky man.'

It was a good weekend for everyone. Keith, who dreamed of older women and had no girl-friend of his own age, was glad to find Tessa's new man unthreatening, quiet, good-tempered, and interested in Tessa in an admiring way that was neither doggy nor too lecherous. The last one she brought here had been obtrusively physical, and had not even bothered to go back to his own room before morning, as Keith discovered when he woke feeling kindly and took Tessa a pot of tea in bed.

The big gift of the weekend was that Matthew, poor, dull, old, dispossessed Uncle Matthew, brought a new friend with him. Lee Foster, a visiting lecturer at his university, was a funny, gutsy American from Boston, who seemed to be as fond of him as he obviously was of her. She was tall and stylish in an unaffected fashion, with a round curly head like a cherub that she turned quickly to take in everything that was going on, adding to it with civilized New England appreciation.

Keith had been fiddling about with some new music, and playing some of his *Three Ring Circus* songs to see what might last and what was now too juvenile. He was already looking forward to immersing himself in the plans of the revue company when he went back to Cambridge in September. He had gone up sporadically for sessions with the ageing adolescent graduate student who was supposed to be his supervisor and had seen some of the maniacs and deviants from the *Circus*, who had promised him he'd be included, if he didn't die.

By now everyone in the house knew 'Time Gone By' like a television jingle. 'Not that again,' Tessa said when he started to sing it quietly on Friday night, playing round the notes instead of on them, and speaking the words. 'Give it a rest, love.'

But Lee Foster got up from Matthew's side and came over to the piano. 'I know that song.' Keith shook his head. 'Sing it again.'

> *'Time gone by . . . played a game.*
> *I'd be leader. All would follow.'*

'Go on.'

> *'Look round now. No one there.*
> *Fingers click on empty air.*
> *Life? It's hollow.'*

Lee joined in the last line. 'I heard that song in a bar in Harvard Square where they do late-night cabaret. A British student sang it.'

'What did he look like?'

'Scrawny, surprised-looking red hair, big nose.'

'John Malchman. I'll kill him.' Keith put his face in his hands. 'Oh, God, look what's happened now, because I couldn't do it in the show.' He dropped his hands into his lap and looked up at Lee. 'It's mine. I wrote it.'

'You *did*? I love it.'

Keith played the tricky, spare little melody, and they sang it together. He began to teach Lee the verse, and Uncle Matthew came over and put his arm round her. She turned her cherub's head quickly to him, and then back to Keith.

> *'Time gone by . . . played a game . . .'*

She was much too young for dear stuffy old Matt, but she was great for him. Keith would be her special young friend, to sing and laugh with.

Agnes was thinking of going on the wagon again. She had clambered on to it many times in her life, because it was not a tumbril to the guillotine. You could fall off it any time you liked. His Lordship William Taylor, of course, would think it was because of what he'd had the arrogance to say to her, so he wouldn't get told. It wasn't because of that anyway. It was because of the way Agnes felt putting her feet to the floor in the mornings, and *she* awake in there, and croaking for her tea. Also, now that the question of pay had come up – for the job of keeper to the senile demented – Agnes was interested.

Ruth had brought in the new slave to the tea parlour to see the old lady: Josephine, whom everybody liked so much, such a good worker. A gallant little widow, they said. Nobody had called Agnes gallant when Edward Mutch died. She had not seen him for fifteen years, and she had only married him in the first place to get rid of the name of Trout – though Mutch was not much of an exchange – but it had felt unpleasant to hear that he had died in far-off Canada on the back seat of a long-distance coach.

Josephine could be a bit hard to stomach in the morning, but she seemed a good-hearted soul. Budgie said 'Come on, Ma' for her, and she took to dropping in now and again on her way to or from work, to cheer up the old lady. Saturday morning she was at the lodge, asking to hear about the old days, which mother loved. They were on about the time when Lady Geraldine died at the beginning of the war, and Sylvia ran the house. Ran it into the ground, you might say.

Ma never talked much about Sylvia, of whom a lot could be said, and Agnes had always been glad that she herself had cut free of the whole mess and got away to sanity when she was demobbed from the ATS in 1946, long before Sylvia buried her old Mr Taylor and went off her nut and let The Sinktuary sink into rack and ruin around her.

'Tell me some more about the war,' Josephine coaxed, 'when you had all those evacuees to look after.'

'My mother never liked them,' Agnes said, 'because they had things in their heads and did their jobs on the floor if you weren't looking.'

'Little devils.' Troutie smiled, for she had liked the children really, soft as she was, and ruined by feudalism to believe that whatever went on at The Sinktuary was all right. 'Put 'em all into the library. When the parents took the kiddies away, we had all those airmen.'

'How *nice*,' said Josephine brightly, as if she were talking to a lunatic or a baby.

'It wasn't.' Troutie chuckled herself into one of those coughs that made Agnes think about giving up smoking, but if you gave up everything, you might as well be dead. 'Never really got that room cleared out, we didn't, after scrubbing, scrubbing. Buckets of suds . . .' She had housework on the brain.

'I heard in the village –' Mrs Josephine had been smarming around those gasbags in the shop and post office, you could be sure – 'that the poor house never really recovered from all that, until Mr and Mrs William took over.'

'What? What do they say?' Troutie opened her leaky eyes wider than usual.

'Well, that Sylvia Taylor became – a bit of a hermit?'

'Bit of what?'

'Closed up most of the house.'

'When? I always took care of it, and she'd say . . .'

'Say what?'

'Eh?'

Josephine was sharp enough to see that she was faking deafness, and Troutie was sharp enough to see that Josephine was prying into what was none of her business. Score: nil-nil.

Jo was getting up to leave the old lady when there were voices outside the room, and William and Matthew Taylor came in with an attractive American woman.

'Hullo, Jo.' William seemed pleased to see Jo in there. 'Glad you've made friends with Mrs Trout. She's my best friend, aren't you, Troutie dear?'

After introducing the American, he and his brother were all over the old lady; Troutie this and that, and, 'Do you remember such and such?' While the American woman talked to the mouldy budgerigar and examined the hundreds of knick-knacks and family pictures, the old lady flirted a bit with her 'Billie'. William and Matthew were like overgrown little boys, back in the nursery with Nanny – the kind of Englishmen who want spotted dick and lumpy custard all their lives.

When Tessa was a child, Troutie must have been about sixty, and still a powerful force at The Sanctuary. With William probably spoiling his daughter and Dorothy being enlightened, this was the kind of security in which Tessa had grown up to see the world as hers for the taking.

Jo said goodbye politely, but Marigold within was working herself up through bitterness towards anger. Tessa had always had everything. Why did she have to have Rex too? Tessa was a creation of her ancestry and upbringing. Marigold was self-made, in every sense of the word. With her father never there and her mother managing the hotel and always tired and irritable, Marigold was expected to grow up early: 'Don't be a cry-baby, be your age, use your head, don't whine, you'll be all right, you're a big girl now'.

She had never been all right. She always felt like a little girl, guiltily, since she knew that was wrong. Rex was the first grown-up who loved the little girl in her. How could she help crashing her whole defenceless being full tilt into his world?

Nannies . . . Daddies . . . Teddies . . . Billie . . . Jo saw Ruth's car in the car park, and turned off behind the stables, past the little paddock with the donkey and goats, and along the rhododendron hedge to the gardens. She was not ready yet to give Ruth a cheerful greeting.

She walked, simmering, on the springy lawn. The cat temple was insufferable, with its sentimental cards pinned up and its pagan goddess degraded into a sort of Christian domesticity. *Who did they think they were*, this family who carried on as if they had exclusive rights to animals?

The Scottish gardener was mowing along the edge of the lake, so Jo ducked between the giant beeches and into the hidden garden, to brood on a bench, helplessly. She got up and looked at the sundial, which told the wrong time. 'Never Too Late for Delight,' it said. The happy people were impregnable.

She bent down, picked up one of their precious totems, the life-size hare with his long paw raised and his ears straight up together like tulip leaves, and hurled it against the wall.

At Sunday lunch, Jill said to William, 'Some news you won't like, I'm afraid.' His daughter-in-law never just told you the news and let you decide for yourself.

'What's that?' he asked tolerantly, carving the cold beef from last night.

'Dennis and I went to the hidden garden to count the goldfish. You know that hare – the very life-like one by the sun-dial?'

'What about it?'

'It's in a flower-bed by the wall, smashed to pieces.'

'Damn,' said William. 'That was a lovely old piece, one of my great-grandparents' originals.'

'I didn't do it,' Dennis put in unnecessarily. 'I bet it was one of the peasants . . . sorry' – he glanced at Keith, from whom he had got the word – 'visitors.'

'They don't do things like that.' His grandfather brought the dish of thinly sliced meat to the table.

'They do everywhere else these days,' Jill said. 'Why not here?'

'Because they don't.'

'You're so trusting,' Jill accused him. 'I'm amazed that half the stuff doesn't get pinched.'

'There's two goldfish missing,' her son put in.

'Dennis . . .' William warned.

After lunch, he went off to inspect the damage. Tessa and Christopher went with him, in case the sculptor could give advice on repairs. The hare was smashed into half a dozen pieces and some small chips.

'Hopeless.' William and Christopher poked about in the flower-bed, picking out all that was left of the graceful hare. 'It could never be repaired,' Chris said. 'But,' he added tentatively, 'if you'd like, I could have a try at making another for you.'

'Could you?' Bit awkward. Chris was a nice chap, the best Tessa had come up with since she had been on her own – suppose he made something ghastly which William couldn't use?'

'If you didn't like it, Daddy,' Tessa read his mind, 'don't worry. Chris makes a lot of animals, and they do sell.'

'Draw me a rough sketch,' Chris said, 'of what you want, and I'll have a go.'

Tessa purred at him. Smiling, William watched them duck under the low door and go off.

He strolled about the gardens, speaking to visitors, answering questions about slugs and delphiniums, and about the circular blue bed round the dwarf spruce, which had plants in it of all cerulean shades from purple to pale sky blue. He tidied away the few cunning weeds in the greenhouse which camouflaged themselves as alpines, and did some dead-heading in Lady Geraldine's rose garden, the long curving bed with hybrid teas and floribundas, backed by standards and arches of climbers, that his grandmother had laid out and he had restored. The staff never seemed to have enough time for that.

Several of the rose bushes had green shoots neatly nipped off by what looked like the teeth of the greedy little muntjack deer, which did an enormous amount of local damage. Perhaps he should at least try George Barton's suggestion; but it did sound daft.

Frank Pargeter had come in by the paying entrance today, with the Venture Club, and would be lucky if he got the chance to sneak off up the hill to where his nightingale fledgelings must be flying by now.

Mr Taylor saw him looking at the family of pintail ducks on the artificial nesting island in the lake.

'Hullo,' he said to Frank. 'You here again?'

'I haven't finished my study on deciduous exotics.' Frank gave his brief cover story.

'Have you seen the fruit coming in on the Acmenia?'

'Ripening nicely,' Frank hazarded. 'I'll be making sketches, but today I'm here with a group. I drive the minibus for the Venture Club.'

'Good,' said Mr Taylor absently. 'Look at this.' He pointed to a mutilated rose bush. 'Muntjack deer. Devils. We've tried spraying, but they think it's salad dressing. They're getting in somewhere. Have to check all the walls and fences again, I suppose.'

And find out where *I'm* getting in, Frank thought.

'One of my staff says I have to hang up hair. Human hair. It's the only thing they hate, apparently.'

'I've heard this, Mr Taylor.'

'Where would one get that?'

'Hairdresser?'

'I couldn't go there.'

'Mrs Taylor?'

'Hers is cut in London by a girl who comes to the flat. I can't see myself prancing in to Faringdon Unisex looking for long hair. They'd think it was some kind of fetish. Do you really think it would work?'

'It would have to be dirty. They need to get the human smell.'

Mr Taylor made a face.

'I don't mind trying for you, if you like,' Frank said.

'You wouldn't?' Mr Taylor's face expanded in pleasure.

'Why not?' Frank wanted to be useful, a welcome visitor to The Sanctuary. He was already doing them a favour by watching and protecting the nightingales, who might perhaps come back next year and for years afterwards, more and more of them, so that on future summer nights the whole tangled copse on the other side of the hill would be filled with music.

Cut 'n' Curl: the sign over the shop was in looped lettering like ringlets, hard to read. The window had a blown-up picture of a sullen girl whose hair had been carefully fashioned to look like a haystack. Cosmetics, scents, a faceless bald head stuck with butterflies on skewers. Women beyond. A counter, chairs, basins, dryers. A man in tight black trousers with hoop earrings.

Frank pushed open the door and plunged in. 'Hullo there,' the man said. (It was a girl.) 'You want a cut?' Her eyes considered what she would do to Frank's wild, woolly hair.

'Oh, no. Thanks. I'm – er, I'm looking for some long hair.'

You what? The girl did not need to say it.

'Yes, you see, long women's hair. I want it for – well, never mind, but I thought you –' *Oh help. Greater love hath no man . . .* 'I thought you might . . .'

'We sometimes sell clients' long hair, for wigs.'

'Oh, I'd buy it. I mean, how much?'

'Full head, twenty pounds.'

'But I only want any old hair. Dirty hair.'

She shook her sleek head at him, the ear-rings flapping like dog's ears. 'It's always washed before cutting.'

A woman reading a magazine, in an armchair so small it would get up with her when she stood up, pushed back the pink metal drying hood and patted her chipolatas of hair. If she had scowled at Frank, he could have stood it, but she smiled at him with sticky frosted lips, and he fled.

He went home and tackled Faye. She was in the back garden, up a step-ladder by the rose arbour, snipping and tidying.

'Fairy.' Sometimes he called her that, since it was the meaning of the name which her parents had given her before they knew she would grow to six feet.

'Frankie.' She had green rose ties in her mouth, like a walrus chewing seaweed.

'You know the geriatric ward at the hospital?'

'Too well.'

'The old ladies – most of them have short hair, don't they? What happens if they come in with it long?'

'The things the man comes out with.' Faye came down from the step-ladder, one large foot shattering a vagrant flower pot. 'They cut it, of course. No time to wash and dry long hair, and it can't be pinned up or plaited, because it makes their old scalps sore.' Faye moved the ladder to the next post.

Frank got a hoe from the toolshed, and ran it between some nearby rows of bush beans. 'They – er, they wash it first?'

'What point in that? I think they just hack it off and throw it away. Frank.' She pulled down a strong arching climber, to tame it to her will. 'When I answer these stupid questions, it's only to humour the homicidal maniac in you.'

'Right,' Frank said cheerfully. 'Any new geriatrics coming in, then?'

'All the time. Hearse at the back door, ambulance at the front. There's always a waiting list.'

'Could I have the hair?' Frank kept his head down, hoeing.

'My lord, Frankie Pargeter, you're kinky! I wonder they let you drive the minibus.'

Carefully, because he had the fish on the hook and was reeling it in, he explained about the Asiatic muntjack deer.

'Just get me one lot, eh, Faye?'

'I can't. Cost me my job, married to a lunatic.'

'I know you will.'

Frank moved along the rows of beans, tranquilly. Faye carried the ladder to the last corner post, stood it down unevenly, and crashed sideways on to a currant bush when she put her foot down on the step.

Frank said, 'There you go,' comfortably. She would not let him pick her up. She would not be dependent.

Within a week Faye had come home from the hospital with a hank of disgusting grey hair in a shopping bag.

'To feed the muntjacks.' She threw it on to the fretted oak table in the hall, and no more was said.

William Taylor put the hair into an onion net and a pair of tights supplied by Jo, and hung them on posts at either end of the big rose bed at the height of a muntjack's nose, about eighteen inches from the ground.

When it was nearly six o'clock, Rob went to the ticket hut to see Mr Archer, who had promised to let him ring the Closing Bell. The end of the rope was too high to reach, so Mr Archer brought his chair out to the tall cypress tree, and Rob stood on that and pealed the sad-sounding bell, once, twice, three times. He would have continued, but Mr Archer, a retired school-master, decreed that more than three pulls would mean you could not ring the bell next time, and Dennis or Annabel would grab the chance.

'Where have you been?' As the last visitors wandered away, Dennis came up out of the cellar door at the side of the house with a bat and an armful of cricket stumps.

'That was me ringing the bell.'

'I might have known. You couldn't hear it, five yards away.'

'How did you know I was ringing it then? Can I play, Dennis?'

'No, because it was my turn to ring the bell and you cheated. Uncle Matthew's going to bowl, and I'm going to teach Lee to bat.' He had to make do with them, because his father had not come this weekend.

Lee and Uncle Matthew were going out to dinner with the other grown-ups, so after a while Dennis came indoors and went up to the top floor to upset Rob, because he was still annoyed about the bell.

'Want to hear something really and truly disgusting?'

'No.' Rob put his hands over his ears. 'Jill!' Jill was in the bathroom with the baby, running water.

'Listen to this,' Dennis said loudly, and Rob loosened his hands a little, in case it was worth hearing. 'You're always on about Flusher, aren't you?' Rob nodded, opening his eyes wide to see Dennis through his curtain of fringe. 'You're so proud of knowing the story, but you've got it all wrong, you know.'

'It's true!'

'That's all you know. Listen, after Phyllis Bunby killed the baby, she didn't flush it away. She – take your hands away – she fed it to the pigs.'

Rob's heart stopped. His legs felt weak. He sat down on the padded playroom fender and got the strength to say, 'Pigs don't eat people.'

'*Don't* they?' Dennis came over and squatted in front of Rob, his jeering face very close. 'What about that old man who escaped from the nursing home and they never found him?'

'What old man?' If there had been a fire in the grate, Rob might have fallen backwards into it.

'Wandered off into a farmyard. Weeks later, they found a pyjama button and his false teeth in the pigsty. Nothing else.'

'I don't believe it.'

'It was in the paper.'

'I don't read the paper.'

'Because you can't read.'

After the Closing Bell rang, Dorothy Taylor came to the tea-room and found Josephine alone. 'Where's Ruth? I wanted to see what time she's coming back to baby-sit.'

'She went off in a hurry ten minutes ago. Her husband came by with her younger son on the way to the hospital. He hurt his ankle falling off his bike – a really bad sprain.'

'Oh dear, she was going to stay with the children while we go out to dinner, but she won't be back. Sunday evening – they'll wait ages in Casualty.'

'Mrs Taylor.' Jo felt herself swelling with pride and nobility, padded breasts and all. 'You know I said I'd help in the house any time . . . let me stay with the children for you.'

'I couldn't.'

'I'd be glad to, honestly. I've got nothing else to do.'

'Well, now . . .' Dorothy was not one to dither about decisions. 'There's only the three bigger ones. My daughter-in-law will take the baby with her. But look – I can't let you do it as a favour.'

'I want to,' Jo said, 'but if it makes you happy,' she felt powerful, 'you can give me what you usually pay Ruth.'

Jo had quite a nice evening. Dennis watched television downstairs. Annabel and Rob had their baths, and then Jo read to them, sitting in the low rocking-chair in the playroom that must have been the nursery during Troutie's reign.

When Annabel stood up to get some juice out of the little upstairs kitchen, she asked Jo pertly, 'Do you dye your hair?'

Well, this was bound to come, however careful she was. Jo had the story ready. 'I've got a bit of grey coming in at the top.'

'My mother doesn't,' Rob said.

'Of course not. She's younger than me.' Jo was proud that her voice was smooth and amiable, though her mind was gritting its teeth. 'I hate the grey at my age, so I colour it in a bit.'

'Read some more.' Rob sat against Jo's legs, warm and bony. *Rex's child!* It was bizarre, part of a wild dream.

When Jo said it was bedtime, Rob and Annabel pretended to be looking for something, and pulled everything out of the toy cupboard.

Shall I make them put it back? They've got to accept me, not resent me. Jo waited a little while and then said, 'Bedtime,' again.

'But you promised I could show you Flusher.'

'Oh, *Rob*,' Annabel protested, and Jo said, 'Not at bedtime.'

'Why not? I'm not afraid. It's just a silly old loo.'

It was. But ugly and somehow fascinating, as a testimonial to Victorian drudgery and slops. Jo could see why a family myth had been built up about it.

She got the children into their rooms. Rob took Charlotte on to his bunk. Annabel had put a large dented celluloid doll into the baby seat, which she put on the foot of her bed. When Dennis came up and listened to music on the stereo in Keith's room, Joe put all the toys and games neatly back in the cupboard and went down to the kitchen to get some supper, as instructed by Dorothy.

The empty house was too big. The high-ceilinged rooms were huge, the arched white corridors branching off to multiple corners and odd levels, the staircase a broad cavern. It ought to be frightening, alone downstairs, but it was friendly and peaceful. Open windows welcomed in night flower scents, and a cool breeze off the lake. Clocks in the hall and drawing-room struck casually, several minutes apart, noting what they thought was the hour melodiously, not recording the relentless passing of time. In the kitchen, china on the tall dresser was a mix of every colour and pattern. The Aga was a faithful, nourishing heart. Someone – Tessa? the daughter-in-law Jill, more likely – had laid out mugs and plates and bowls for the children's breakfast.

Jo took her sandwich upstairs, and read a book in the nursery. Dennis said he could stay up until the grown-ups came back, and at ten years old Jo was not going to argue with him; but after the music stopped, she looked into the room and found him asleep on Keith's bed.

This house is mine, saith the Josephine. When the telephone rang, it was Ruth, apologetic and grateful.

'Simon all right?' Jo asked.

'He will be. They gave him something for the pain and swelling. *Thanks*, Jo. You are a dear.'

Yes, aren't I?

When the phone rang again, Jo answered it efficiently.

'Tessa?' A man's voice. What if it had been Rex? Would he have known Marigold through Jo's new, louder, more assertive voice?

'No, it's the baby-sitter. Can I take a message? Call Colin? Right. I'll tell her.'

Bad luck, Col, me old sport. I think she's quite busy with the beard.

Jo went into the cabin to look at Rob steamily asleep, the little dog limp under his outflung arm. Then she went back to Troutie's rocking-chair in the nursery and gloated. In charge of the children, in charge of the phone line coming in from the outer reaches, in charge of the huge house at the centre of the world.

In charge of Rob.

When Tessa and Jill returned, Tessa took Charlotte from

Rob's bunk, and Jill took the baby seat from Annabel's bed, unwound the baby blanket from the naked doll and threw it in the toy cupboard.

Jo put her book back on the shelves by the housemaid's closet and followed them downstairs. There was a pot of tea going in the kitchen, but she declined gracefully. There might come a time when she would sit round the kitchen table with her employers, but it was not yet.

Next afternoon the chatty clatter of cream teas was shredded by a high-pitched screaming from the garden side of the house. Cups were put down. Some people stood up. Voices shouted, a dog was barking.

'What on earth?' Ruth pelted out across the yard and through a door in the wall that led round to the gardens.

Jo piloted the tea-room into calm, like the captain of a panic-struck jumbo jet, but some of the younger visitors went off to find the excitement. When the cash slips were tallied later, a few of them had not come back to pay.

The screaming died down. There was no more shouting. Ruth came back, red in the face and wiping her glasses on her apron.

'Everything's all right.' She smiled and nodded. More tea was poured, jam and clotted cream bowls scraped, new visitors wandered in and found a place to sit. 'Cream tea, Doris?' 'Oh, I shouldn't.'

When they could get a moment together in the scullery, Ruth told Jo. 'Poor little Rob. Screaming his head off. Hysterical, I've never seen anything like it. He was up at one of the top windows, and if it hadn't been for the bars, I swear he'd have thrown himself out.'

'What happened?' Jo ran the taps to cover their voices.

'That Dennis. Played him a horrible trick. His grandpa won't half give it him, silly little devil.'

Chapter Eight

It was only a joke. Last night Jo had stuffed the dented celluloid doll upside down into the thick porcelain bowl of The Flusher, patent 1882. Only a joke, but the results were far more violent than she had expected. The screams and pandemonium and shouting had been quite stimulating, with the censuring of Dennis to complete the satisfaction.

What's next? Jo had no plans. She was here. That was enough for now. She would see what came up, as the chance of the doll had turned up – a better reward than the ten pounds Dorothy Taylor had pressed on her for baby-sitting.

Jo continued to look in on Mary Trout now and again, cultivating her image of being kind to old ladies, and hoping for titbits of inside information about the family.

One Monday afternoon, Agnes had gone to have her feet seen to and Ruth was at the lodge, fussing and clucking over her grandmother.

'We were talking about old times,' she said (as if the old Trout ever talked of anything else). She had pushed the old lady over to the back window, so that she could get the air without the breeze, and she brought up another chair for Jo to sit by her.

The old lady nodded and chuckled. She was evidently having a good day.

'My mother's late back.' Ruth looked at the flowered china clock. 'And I've got to get to the shops.'

It had worked before with the children. It worked now. 'I'd be glad to stay here for a while,' Jo said.

'Oh, no, you can't always be doing things for me.'

'We do things for each other, Ruth. You're always helping me – with the baking, and that time the fat man had a fit and I didn't know what to do, and taking me to the fabric place for the curtain material. Besides, I like talking to your grand-mother.' She raised her voice.

Tessa stopped in at the lodge after leaving Rob with his grandparents. She was wearing a mouth-watering creamy suit that would have looked like death on Marigold, but looked fantastic on glowing, tanned Tessa.

One day, Marigold thought, I shall put my two capable hands round her neck and squeeze the babbling, cocksure life out of her ... Would that be enough? If Tessa were dead, she would not suffer.

Tessa talked to Troutie about coming to The Sanctuary as a child; Troutie would show her the attic store-rooms and let her take old dresses and fancy hats downstairs to give a perform-ance.

'Always putting on a show, you was.' Troutie had refused to talk to Jo, but she maundered and mumbled away to Tessa. 'Lovely you was, in Lady Geraldine's frock with the glittery beads. My golden girl, I called you.'

'I called you Toutie.' Tessa bent to kiss her. 'I still love you best of anyone. Am I still your golden girl?'

Sickening stuff. Troutie put up a lizard's hand and patted Tessa's face. Pat, pat, mumble, mumble. Jo would have liked to throw a bucket of water over the pair of them.

When Tessa had pranced out, Jo tried to get Mary to drop the winsome-old-retainer front and remember some of the truth.

'Rob showed me the cellars, Mrs Trout. So cold, even in

July. How did you stand it, working down there? The fireplace in the servants' hall is a joke, and that great old scullery – like an ice box.'

'Near the kitchen range.' The old lady chuckled, gasped and coughed. 'Then you was too hot.'

'I've seen all over the house, you know. It must have made a shocking lot of work for all of you, being so big and grand.'

'Local jobs,' Troutie said quite clearly and sharply. Her leathery hands fiddled with the musty stuff of her skirt.

Since she would not remember anything Jo said – she remembered nothing from less than twenty years ago – Jo risked the comment, 'But what a waste of lives spent catering to a few rich people.'

'This was my home.' The rusty voice started strong, quavered, and was swamped by that waterlogged cough.

Jo made herself a cup of tea, which tasted slightly flawed, as if Agnes had poisoned the water. In the newspaper she found an advertisement for the kind of small unfinished dresser she wanted, to paint for her kitchen. Now that she knew she was going to stay for some time, for as long as it took, it was worth making improvements at Bramble Bank.

Agnes was in a bad mood when she came home and found Jo there instead of Ruth.

'Poking your face in where you're not wanted,' was her theme. She walked aimlessly from the back room to the front, lighting cigarettes. When Jo hid the lighter in her own pocket, Agnes lit one cigarette from the last, leaving sourly smoking stubs in saucers. No wonder her mother's chest was like a sewer.

Troutie was very deeply asleep. 'You can go then, can't you,' Agnes said, as an order, not a suggestion.

'I thought I – shall I just help you to put her to bed?'

'She's all right there for a bit. Leave me alone, can't you? I'm tired.'

Sloshed, more like. Agnes had come home aggressive and unsteady, knocking into the door frame.

'Perhaps you should take a nap too.'

'Mind your own business.'

But Agnes did go upstairs, stumbling on the stair rods and banging her bedroom door savagely. Jo took the newspaper with the advertisement and left. Walking up the drive to where she had left her bicycle, she smouldered about the two of them. Agnes was vilely offensive. Troutie was vilely irritating, with her old pensioner boot-licking. Lady Geraldine. Miss Sylvia. Tessa – oh, always Tessa. My golden girl.

Chafing, too restless to go home, Jo turned off the road, down a lane to where the remains of an old burial barrow rose smoothly among grazing sheep. From the top you could see villages and farms, the lazily curling Lynn river, and the dark mass of The Sanctuary, with a glint of the lake through trees. Jo sat among the spirits of ancient Britons, arms braced and hands clenched on the turf.

She would return while Troutie slept, and tap at the window to frighten her – tap and duck down among the bushes. No one would see, because the old lady was not at her usual window by the drive. Reach up with a stick and bang on the window, and be gone before Agnes looked out.

Start a little fire outside the open window, make some smoke, so that Troutie would wake and think the house was on fire. 'Agnes! Aggie!' 'What do you want?' 'Fire – oh, help!' 'Shut your noise.'

Jo rode back towards The Sanctuary, the plan shifting back and forth in her head. One moment, it looked perfect, the next, it looked silly. Give it up? Then she'd never know if it would have worked.

She left her bicycle in the courtyard and unlocked the tea-room. If anyone questioned her being here, she could be doing some extra jobs, good zealous Jo. She took the postcards and souvenir mugs and garden guides off the display table and put a bowl of soapy water on it. Then she went through the door in the wall and made her way behind the carriage house and hay barn to the back garden of the lodge cottage, where the casement window stood half open on to the neglected vegetable bed and fruit bushes.

She had brought the newspaper with her. She crouched down between the house and the bushes, crumpled up a couple of sheets, and lit them with Agnes's cigarette lighter. They burned quite well, and caught some of the dry grass, which sparked and smouldered. There was not enough smoke. It diffused and spread before it reached the window. Jo crumpled two or three more pages together, lit them in her hand, and on an impulse that brought the same sense of release as hurling the accursed stone hare at the wall, she half stood up and threw the burning paper ball through the window. She pitched the cigarette lighter in after it, and fled.

Coming back to the tea-room, she found Rob, riding his old bicycle that was too small for him round the yard.

'You promised.' He put down his feet, and dragged them to a stop on the cobbles.

'Promised what?'

'To come and see where the horses were burned up in the foaling stable.'

Jo had not planned what she was going to do. She might find someone and ask whether they smelled smoke. She might not. She felt perfectly serene. It did not matter what she did, so she might as well go with Rob, to please him.

'Get away from the range.' Cook fussed and glared, brandishing a long two-pronged fork like the devil's prodder.

'Them carrots is done.'

'What about the sprouts?'

Little Mary wanted to stay by the throbbing stove, not go back to the cold muddy sink water in the freezing scullery.

'Useless child.'

Mrs Belcher yanked open the oven door on a blast of heat and roasting fumes that rushed out to sizzle Mary's eyebrows and fill her throat with greasy smoke.

'Told you to get away!'

Mary gasped and coughed, bent double, sank, and disappeared from the underground kitchen scene, which went heedlessly on without her.

'The shed was here,' Rob told Jo. 'Look – you can see the black scorch marks on the wall. The mother horse was inside with her foal. They could still hear them kicking and screaming, but they couldn't let them out. People still hear the screams, you know.'

He looked at Jo to see if she would swallow this. She wasn't listening. She turned quickly and ran from him along the back of the carriage house. She was running towards where someone was screaming and shouting.

Rob fell into a black hole of panic, terrified, alone. He ran out on to the drive, screaming for his grandmother. People were running, someone shouted, 'Fire!'

'Granny!'

They were running down the drive, to where thick smoke was coming out of the lodge. His grandmother was there. She took his hand and tried to pull him indoors. He broke free and ran round the side of the house.

When the fire engine came flashing and wailing, Rob was standing in a wheelbarrow by the cypress tree, ringing the Closing Bell, ringing, ringing, with no one to stop him.

Chapter Nine

William had been in Shropshire with the Tenant Farmers' Union, discussing changes in landlord–tenant agreements. When Dorothy telephoned, he started home at once.

Troutie *dead*? It had been possible for years, but now it wasn't possible. He had already bought her ninetieth birthday present. Shocked, and driving too fast, he remembered walking past the lodge window where she slept like a pile of wheezing old clothes and thinking, she might be better off dead. Now that she was, he wanted her alive in any shape. How easily we sentence even those we love – better to die, had a good long life; why struggle to reach ninety? He was ashamed of that thought, so lightly and stupidly tossed off, but he could not escape it, as if poor old Troutie sat beside him in the car, chiding, 'See what you done, you naughty boy!'

By the time Agnes had woken to the smell of the fire, her mother had been suffocated by the toxic fumes given off by her smouldering foam-filled chair. Budgie was dead too, but no one noticed that, until one of the firemen brought his cage out of the swamped, wrecked room.

Agnes had been angry when she saw the bird. 'Why didn't he call me?' She took the small feathered body out of the cage and glared at it in the palm of her hand. 'All those years of driving me mad with, "Come on Ma!" Would it have killed you to call out to me?'

Someone had muttered, 'It killed him not to.' Probably Keith.

Two policemen came to The Sanctuary next morning.

A saucer of cigarette stubs, a lighter, a scrap of newspaper, not quite burned. Nobody needed to say that these things pointed to Agnes.

'I was up in my bedroom.' She sat with her hair wild, eyes baleful and jaw stuck out, although no one had accused her of anything. 'Laying down.'

'Did you get up and come down for a cigarette at some time?'

'No, I – well, I don't know. How should I know?' She rubbed a hand through her disordered hair. 'I was tired. I went up to lay down, that's all I know.'

'That's right.' Jo was present at the meeting in the hall: police caps on the oak chest with the magazines and visitors' book, lilies overpowering, roses massed in the big Coalport bowl on the centre table. 'She was going upstairs as I left.'

'And that would be – when, Mrs – er?'

'Kennedy. Between three-thirty and four, I suppose. I went off on my bike to Green Barrow. As I came back, the stable clock was chiming five – it's slow – and I met the little boy, Rob, in the yard.'

'Why did you come back, Jo?' Dorothy Taylor asked. 'It wasn't a working day.'

'I thought I'd clean the souvenir table, while I had the time. But Rob took me out behind the stables to show me something. Then I heard someone scream.'

'Who was that?'

'Agnes, I suppose. Mrs Mutch.'

'You'll all say it was my fault.' Poor Agnes, muddled and in a state of shock, looked round belligerently.

No one contradicted this, but no one confirmed it. They

made comforting noises, and Ruth put her short strong arms round her mother and said, 'Don't carry on.'

The policeman's report would cite, 'Possible careless use of smoking materials.' At the inquest later, the coroner gave an open verdict. There were no charges, but local gossip, never favourable to Agnes, made plenty of unofficial ones.

Ruth was terribly upset. She did not come to work next day. William took the dogs across the river and through the water-meadow to her cottage outside Lynnford, partly because he felt so rotten, partly because he knew Ruth did. They wallowed together in the pit of blaming themselves. Ruth was usually so calm and down-to-earth, whatever happened. It was not like her to be hysterical, but when William came and put his arms round her in great sorrow, she sobbed and cried out and would not be comforted for quite a long time.

When she was quieter, William stood up and said he would make tea, and headed vaguely for the kitchen.

'No, I'll do it, Will.' Old habit got Ruth to her feet, glasses off, face swollen and watery, little nose red. William followed her and sat at the small table by the windowsill geraniums, while Ruth moved about with something more like her old bustle, sluicing her face at the sink and wiping it on the roller towel.

'Maids of honour. Gran liked them.' She put a plate of little cakes by William's mug that said 'Happy Mother's Day, 1977'. She and William looked across the table at each other, with their mouths drawn down. 'I got the almonds yesterday, and made – I made them for – for –'

'I know. You always thought of her.'

'Don't, Will. I'm done crying. But who will I make little treats for now, till those silly boys grow up and give me grandchildren?'

'She was – like a child to you, you mean?'

'As she got old. Wasn't she to you?'

William thought, then shook his head, chewing the almond cake without tasting it. 'She – all my life, really – was more like my mother.'

Tessa came rushing to The Sanctuary as soon as the news reached her. She went to look at the ruined room, and wanted to go and look at Troutie in the mortuary, but Dorothy restrained her. After Ruth and William had stopped blaming themselves, Tessa started it up again.

Agnes had gone to her friend in Swindon to avoid the talk, so since Tessa could not take it out on her, she blamed her father and Ruth – for allowing a foam-filled chair; for leaving Agnes in charge, which had worked all right for several years, 'when we all knew she was a wino'.

'Not that bad,' William said. 'And I had it out with her last month, you know, and I really thought she would cut down.'

'You believed that, of course.'

This uncomfortable conversation was taking place in the kitchen, while Jo was in the baking pantry, scrubbing at this morning's bowls and beaters and baking tins.

When William began mildly, 'Well, I hoped that she –' Jo felt moved to come to the doorway and say, 'I don't want to butt in, and I haven't told anyone this, but perhaps I'd better say that I did think Agnes was a bit – you know, when she came back that evening.'

'But she wasn't drinking then,' William said. 'She told me the chiropodist had cut her feet about a bit, and she felt groggy. That was why she went up to lie down.'

'We-ell . . .' Jo raised her black eyebrows.

Fiery Miss Tessa rounded on her. 'Then how dared you leave her with poor Troutie?' Outraged golden girl.

Before Jo could make the mistake of firing back, 'How dare *you* speak to me like that?', William said, 'Come on, Tess, we all of us left it like that, for too long.'

'I wouldn't have, if I'd been here.'

'You *were* here. A lot. But you weren't the one who tackled Agnes about her drinking. I was.'

'Our hero.'

Back in the bakery, Jo thought: How very interesting. A little rift in the cosy father–daughter love affair? Nothing like sudden death to stir things up.

'I'll never forget it,' Jo said to Mr and Mrs Richardson, when they came round to Bramble Bank to commiserate with her, and to get some inside information. 'The little boy was showing me the remains of the old stable where a mare and foal were burned to death years ago. "Oh, that's dreadful," I said, and he said, "Yes, and now the place is haunted." "Are you sure?" I said.' The Richardsons liked dialogue stories. '"People still hear the screaming now," he said, and just at that moment, I heard Mrs Mutch scream.'

'What did you do, Josephine?' The Richardsons were having a lager in Jo's now habitable garden, the wooden seats unsteady on the rough flat stones her weeding had discovered outside the back door.

'I ran down to the lodge. I'll never forget it. Never.'

'Poor old lady,' Mr Richardson said. 'Lived there ages, hadn't she?'

'All her life, just about.'

'Nice that she should die there then,' said Mrs Richardson, who quite liked a death, as long as it wasn't hers.

Right for her to die there. Right for her to die. When the Richardsons had gone Jo went upstairs and looked at herself in the mirror behind the cupboard door.

'Murderess.'

She tried it out to see what it would do to her face. The face remained calm and enquiring.

'I killed an old lady.'

But Jo's painted face remained alert and cool and quite attractive, and the Marigold behind it did not feel anything, now that the keyed-up, impulsive excitement was long spent.

'You're sick,' Jo told this face, of which she was getting quite fond, 'you know that?'

But the face smiled confidently, and she felt full of energy, and really very well. She felt better than she had in all the years since that nightmare April when Marigold was nursing the joyful secret of her pregnancy, and Rex had come home from work, calmly taken off his jacket and poured himself a drink and said without turning round, 'I may as well tell you now. I've been seeing a girl called Tessa Taylor. She's the woman I've been looking for all my life. I'm going to live with her.'

Through friends, Marigold had found out about Tessa and her family, and a few days later, she drove through drenching rain to The Sanctuary. She had no definite plans. She was sick and desperate. She knew the gardens were open. She would prowl there, spy on the family, look through windows, see without being seen.

The motorway ran like a swirling stream. Trucks kicked up fountains of dirty spray. It took longer to get to Lynnford than she had expected, and when she reached The Sanctuary, the garden entrance was just closing.

'Please let me in.' The gate was one more direct rebuff. Every way she turned, her life was blocked.

'I'm sorry.' The ticket man shook his head.

'Just for ten minutes.'

A grey car left the front of the great house and circled the drive. The ticket man turned up his coat collar, called, 'Good-night Mr Taylor!' and walked away.

Marigold dashed out on to the drive and grabbed at the driver's side of the car, beating her palm on the window. The car stopped. The window went down. The middle-aged man and the small woman beside him looked at Marigold in her soaked khaki raincoat, her pale hair plastered across her face.

'What do you want? What is this?'

'I want to see Tessa Taylor.'

'She's not here,' the man said. 'Why don't you telephone, and – '

'Mr Taylor.' Marigold clutched the top of the window glass with cold wet fingers to stop him raising it. 'Listen to me. Your daughter – I've got to tell you what your daughter – what she – what your daughter's doing!' She was babbling and incoherent, half blind, slobbering through tears and rain.

'Whatever it is you want,' the woman spoke without leaning towards Marigold, upright, dismissive, 'we can't discuss it. I must ask you to leave. We're late for an appointment.'

'Come on,' the man said, more kindly. 'Let me take you to your car.'

He began to open the door, and Marigold stumbled back. Speechless, she turned and ran from them over the drive, the sodden raincoat flapping round her legs. Behind her, she heard the door shut and the car move slowly on the gravel.

When she reached her own car, she saw that the Taylors' car was waiting for her to leave. God damn them. If they had physically thrown her out, she could not have felt more humiliated.

Through her misted rear window as she reached the arch over the entrance, she saw the grey car following. She drove away fast, devastated, her vision blurred by tears and the streaming windscreen.

God damn and curse them. When Marigold later hit a car in front as it slowed down, it was *their* fault, Tessa Taylor's fault, the fault of all of them – the tinkle of glass, the angry driver, her bruising plunge against the seat-belt – out of her control, inevitable.

Jo's face in the bedroom mirror went on smiling. Inevitable that she had come back. It had taken a long time, but seven years had only strengthened the resolution of her revenge.

'You're depressed,' Dottie diagnosed William.

'Aren't you?'

'Yes, but Troutie doesn't need me now, and those children at the home do, so I'm going to deal with it by going to work, and you'd better do the same.'

'Don't be brisk with me, Dottie.'

William was really depressed. Troutie disappearing God knew where, to starch tablecloths and make Yorkshire pudding and paint wooden dolls and all the things she'd loved to do, had left an enormous chasm at the centre of his being. When Dottie had driven off in her neat little dusty car, which he had promised to wash for her and forgotten, he was drawn, inevitably, to the nursery.

He trod too heavily up the stairs for a man of fifty-five, and went slowly along the top corridor to the square sunny room at the end. His heart was heavy. That was exactly what it felt like. All the old emotional clichés described actual physical sensations. A broken heart. When Suzanne threw him over, before he met Dottie, something inside his chest was shattered, like a vase cracked all over. My heart aches. After Angela's son was killed, there was a pain in his chest like pleurisy, or a badly bruised rib. Heavy-hearted. He moved slowly now, because he was carrying a leaden weight.

A few of the old knick-knacks were still on the mantelpiece. The clock with the funny face. The fat-backed Staffordshire dog, chipped now, its smooth head and spaniel ears much licked. The earthenware mug that used to hold pencils and blunt-ended scissors. In Troutie's day there had been a motto on an oval china plaque that leaned against the wall. It said something very significant, he could not remember what, but Troutie had set store by it, and quoted it often enough to give it biblical truth.

Perhaps Troutie would like it now. He could have it set into the middle of his funeral wreath, and drop it into her grave. He got the key and went into the attic store-room, rummaging about among mirrors, lamps, conch shells, photographs, souvenir mugs, boxes of papers and books, the old train set. He ought to get that out for Rob.

In a basket among some of the nursery stuff – a baby's hairbrush, a light-up Father Christmas, part of a doll's tea-set – he found the brown Devon china plaque upside down in a biscuit tin with a royal wedding on the lid. He turned it over. It said, 'Tis a long lane that 'as no turnin'.' Only that, after all? Disappointed, he put it back in the tin.

When he went up to London, he wanted to ring Angela and tell her about Troutie. Before he could decide, he got a call from her, at the office.

'I took a chance on finding you there. Will, I – look, could you possibly meet me somewhere when you're free?'

She came to the Chelsea flat. 'I need to talk to someone about Peter,' she said quietly. 'Could you stand it?'

Less than three months after her son's death, Angela was finding that people expected her to be getting back to normal. Ralph had never wanted to hear much about it, and even women friends who had let her talk and weep and rage at first were showing signs that they wished she would talk about something else.

She talked and William listened, and forgot to worry about saying the right things. She was so muted and vulnerable, and he was so honoured that she had come here, that some of the pain of poor Troutie faded already, even though he hardly spoke of her.

Before Angela left, they arranged to meet again.

'Not because of Peter.' She kissed him softly. 'Just for you and me.'

Troutie's funeral had to wait until after the inquest. Meanwhile, they had a burial ceremony for Budgie before Tessa and Rob went home.

Ruth was there, and her younger son, and Polly Dix with her two small daughters. Rob carried the bird, in a sugar packet wrapped in Christmas paper, behind the back wall of the hidden garden to the pet cemetery, where favourite animals had been buried ever since Walter and Beatrice Cobb turned Lynnford Place into The Sanctuary.

There were some tablets set in the wall, and irregular rows of small mossed-over headstones. You could read only a few of the inscriptions: 'Little Billie, a merry monkey, "Form'd of joy and mirth",' from whom Troutie had taken William's nickname. 'Nemo, good stable cat.' 'Champion, soft mouth, soft heart.' 'Champion, killed in action by Royal Mail van.' 'Champion, friend of Will, 1945–53.'

William dug a small hole deep enough to foil dogs. Troutie's great-grandson laid the red and gold package in it, because Rob wouldn't, and William filled in the earth and marked the spot with a wide plant label on which was written, 'Budgie, beloved bird of Mary Trout.' Tessa had promised Rob that she would get a little headstone engraved in the Goldhawk Road.

At Troutie's funeral a week later, almost all the close family were there. All the Sanctuary staff came, and people from several villages, retired postmen and tradesmen who had known Mary Trout for years, two district nurses, and all her descendants, including Agnes's two brothers, one spry, one ponderous, who had not lifted a finger for the old lady, but immediately attacked Agnes for not having put 'our mother' into a nice safe nursing home.

The funeral procession was to start at 1.30, but William, who should have been at a board meeting in London, was tied up with a long phone call, and so the first few garden visitors were coming along the cypress walk as they set out from the house with Mary Trout's short coffin, borne by William, Matthew, Rodney, Keith, George Barton and Agnes's spry brother.

At Ruth's request, Troutie was carried along the round-about path to the church, where long ago the servants were made to walk to service behind the tall laurels, so that guests in the great house would not see them.

'As a reminder of the bad old days?' Keith had asked Ruth. 'To make us descendants feel ashamed?'

'I had hoped being so ill would make you less rude,' his mother Harriet said.

Ruth said, 'Don't be daft, Keith. It's because my Gran liked to remember how she and another young maid used to hang back on Sunday to giggle at the cook and housekeeper dressed up in their best corsets, and the stable boys would wait in the hedge and catch them at the corner.'

Visitors strolling along the spectacular perennial border stopped to look at the small procession crossing the lawn from the corner of the house and disappearing behind the line of laurels. One of the intriguing aspects of The Sanctuary was that the place was not just a preserved relic. There was family life – and apparently death – going on here every day, so a visitor could feel part of the whole scene, not just an observer.

As the mourners emerged from the laurel walk, cars on the road could see them treading slowly along the path beyond the fence of the pony paddock. The gate in the churchyard wall was always locked, so that no one could get in to the gardens that way. The vicar now waited there with the key, to make the symbolic gesture of admitting Mary Trout into the hereafter.

Frank Pargeter, dropping easily down the hill from the copse with a buoyant heart, stopped on the stone bridge across the river and respectfully took off the green baseball cap with the long peak that shaded his binoculars when he was watching birds against the sun.

The fledgling nightingales were flying now. Frank had spotted two of the youngsters in their juvenile plumage, larger than the last sight of them before he went off to Scotland for Faye's holiday. Frank's life was considered to be one long glut of leisure since he retired, so a trip was always known as Faye's holiday. She had attended a choir festival in Inverness. Frank had seen, on an island in a small lake, a pair of red-necked phalarope.

When the funeral cortège – not a tragic passing, Frank hoped, since he felt very concerned about this family – had gone through the gate towards the church, he crossed the bridge and went round the lake to inspect Lady Geraldine's rose garden. Had those shameless muntjack deer dared to make inroads on the tender shoots while he had been away?

The rose bushes still looked in fine condition. White, yellow, apricot, deep red, all shades of pink, the heavy blooms were hanging on to their heartbreaking summer beauty. The air was giddy with their fragrance. No deep dents of little cloven hooves in the clean, turned earth. Hanging from a post at one end, the horrible old hair was still stuffed into a limp pair of cream tights. At the other end of the rose bed, it hung in a long net, stringy hanks of it escaping through the mesh, grey wisps fluttering from the top.

Well done, Frank. William Taylor and his wife must bless

thy name, as they come lovingly here with trug and secateurs to gather roses for the house. Well done, Faye and the geriatric ward.

Rob had fidgeted through the church service, with his mother on one side and Dennis on the other. Dennis knew how to behave in church, because his school had its own chapel. Rob never went to church, except on Mothering Sunday, when his mother liked to see him collect a small posy of daffodils at the altar and bring them angelically back to her.

Dennis kept jabbing Rob with his elbow and telling him to shut up.

'Is Troutie in that box?' Rob whispered, under cover of the last hymn.

'Clot,' Dennis muttered. 'When you die, you go away for ever.'

'Where?'

'Hell,' Dennis said nastily.

So the sinister box that had been carried down the laurel path by Wum and Uncle Matthew and Uncle Rodney and George and Keith and a strange little bald man like a gnome was empty. What trick was this?

'*Where is Troutie?*' he asked his mother, as soon as she took him out of the church with Annabel, because they weren't to go to the graveside.

'Darling, you know.'

'In hell.'

'No, in heaven.'

'She's in the box, silly,' Annabel said.

In the box, not in the box . . . what were they hiding from him? On the way back to the house, Annabel peeled off to the pony field, and Rob peeled off in the other direction. After being stuck in the crowded pews, he wanted to be by himself.

He took off his shoes and paddled about at the edge of the marsh, finger-trawling for minnows.

'What are you doing?' Jo was there with a basket.

'Nothing.'

'Come up to the rose garden with me. I'm going to cut some roses for the tea table.'

Flowers did not mean anything in Rob's life, although everyone here made such a fuss about them, but he would take some yellow blooms to his mother, who was a bit droopy today, like everyone else.

At the end of the long flower-bed, which was shaped like an S, for Sanctuary, there was a post, and on the post at the height of Rob's eyes something very horrid hung and swung in the breeze. A long, twisted, terrible grey something.

'*What's that, Jo?*'

She was in the middle of the flower-bed, cutting roses with the snippers. 'Looks like poor Troutie's hair, doesn't it?' She did not look up.

Troutie's hair. All that was left of her. And in a gulping shock that brought vomit up into his mouth, Rob knew why Troutie was not in the box in church . . . because, like Phyllis Bunby's baby, they had fed her to the pigs!

Chapter Ten

If Rob were my child – Jo had taken to thinking in terms like
that – I wouldn't have taken him to the funeral. Stupid, selfish
Tessa probably had some half-baked ideas about small children
being introduced to death, or else she wanted him along for
adornment, his grey trousers and white shirt complementing
the mauve and white dress she had probably bought specially
for this non-occasion.

There had been far too much emotional fuss and hysteria
about the death of an eighty-nine-year-old woman who had
been spared a longer decay. No wonder the child had gone
over the top again. This was getting to be quite a feature of
Sanctuary opening hours. Visitors would come to expect
screams for their entry money.

Tessa went back to London, which lessened the tension.
When she was here, Jo was alert to find out more about her.
Knowledge is power. She watched for glimpses of Tessa,
listened to her voice on the tennis court, hoped she would pay
one of her slumming visits to the tea-room:

'Goodness you're busy – want any help? Ruth, if I could
make fruit cake like you, I'd die happy. Can I sneak a scone?'

'Hul*lo*! Enjoying your tea? I *am* glad. Seen the gardens, have
you? Yes, I know, a lot of walking. You've earned a cream tea,
I'd say.'

Jo's job now was to get herself well in with the family, not only as the tea-room treasure, but perhaps, as time went on, an indispensable member of the household. It would take time, because if she pushed, they would resent her, but she had all the time in the world. What else did she have to do?

After Rex abandoned her, one of the bad things for Marigold had been that she had nothing she needed to do. She could have gone back to work. The school was always short of staff, but she could not face teaching, and she did not need to, thanks to the sale of the hotel when her mother died, and the London house that Rex had made over to her, plus panic payment for his freedom.

The worst thing had been having nobody to look after. For almost ten years she had lived for Rex, worked to support him while he was clawing his way up the financial ladder from nothing, done everything his way – looked and talked and behaved like the woman he wanted her to be, which he then used to condemn her when he didn't need her any more.

Nothing to do, and no one to look after. In the seven years since Rex walked out, Marigold had taken some museum courses and learned to do a few more things with her skilful hands, like calligraphy and mending fine china. But who needed her? No one. She did some volunteer work, but children were too painful, and old people too boring, and fund-raising too frustrating. Nothing she did engaged her, because all this time she was so fixated on her rage against Tessa, which had grown sharper when she heard about Rob's birth, that she could not connect with other people, nor take their problems or interests seriously. The anger gnawed at her, and grew fat on her substance.

When she heard through one of the few friends she still saw from the old days that Tessa had dumped Rex, rage over-whelmed her. What kind of an evil bitch is this, who steals a husband, gets a baby, and calmly walks out when it suits her?

Tessa Taylor, the arch-enemy, the fiend, the legion of demons, her and her wretchedly secure family, Tessa and her beloved child, who was Rex's son.

So Marigold had become Jo, to infiltrate the enemy camp. She watched and listened, and lost no opportunities to please. Ruth gave her a small salary increase, because she was working longer hours. Dorothy Taylor found herself employing Jo to do a few little extra jobs, like shopping or feeding the dogs and cats if everyone was out.

William, a man who seemed easily moved to both happiness and sorrow, was still downcast after his precious Troutie's death, but he warmed to Jo's enthusiasm for the gardens, and her desire to learn. She read a book on alpines, so that she could be intelligent in the greenhouse, and when he went to Saudi Arabia to see a client, he asked Jo to visit the alpine house every day to check the ventilation and watering.

'I don't want to go away,' William told Dorothy, 'even for a couple of days.'

'Do you good, Will, a change of scene, and a bit of luxury living.'

'I'd rather be here with you.'

He must have looked like this sometimes when he was a child.

'It's been sad for you here, love,' Dottie said.

'Everything was going well – and then, poor Troutie ... what next, Dottie? All's not well.'

'Oh, come on, Will.' She kissed him, and rubbed her cheek upwards against his, to lift his rumpled face into a smile. 'It will be all right, you'll see. All *is* well. The family is fine. The gardens are more beautiful than ever. Don't you love to see people wandering about so happily, finding their peace here, wherever they come from? The rest of the summer is going to be great, and you always love the Festival of the Lake. Nat Archer says entrance money is up from this time last year, and Ruth and Jo are doing excellent business in the tea-room.'

'Jo's such a good worker.' William smiled. 'Loves the garden, too, and keen to learn. She's going to keep an eye on my alpines while I'm away. She's a big help.'

Dorothy was at the clinic almost every day, but in the evenings while William was away she worked at the slow, intermittent job of painting the library, which had not been refurbished or used since she and William had taken over the house in the late seventies. She had finished the window frames and sills and was working on the two sets of double doors, and the panelled space between the outer and inner doors, originally designed to keep heat in and house noises out.

When Jo found out that this was one of Dorothy's many projects, she came forward, in her Josephine style, all firm pointed bosoms and dark curving hair swinging round her face.

'I'd like to help, if you'd let me. I love to paint,' she said in the rather stagey voice she used when she was not sure how something was going to be received.

Dorothy's instinct was to decline, because she liked to work and think by herself, but with limited free time the work in the long tall room was going too slowly, because of the elaborate eighteenth-century mouldings and the intricate woodwork of the glass-fronted shelves.

She waited before answering, then took a breath to help her to say with enthusiasm, 'Of course, Jo, if you'd really like to. I'd love to have some help.'

The free walls, patched with the ghosts of departed portrait frames, were going to be painted the colour of red dessert apples. The high plaster frieze would all have to be cleaned and repainted some day.

The library was still in a fairly depressing state, the wood floor dirty and scarred, the walls stained, the air musty and stale, in spite of open windows and the fresh paint.

'Funny old smell in here,' Jo said to Dorothy, as they worked quite companionably, on each side of one of the high panelled doors.

'It's the old books, I'm afraid. They've been so neglected, and this room was always damp.'

'The leather bindings need proper treatment, I expect.'

'I haven't got time to do that, and I don't know how,' Dorothy said from the outer side of the door. 'It would cost the earth to get someone to come in and do it professionally.'

'Perhaps I could do a few books for you some time?'

'It's quite a difficult job, I think.' Dottie paused, gilding her way round a moulded wreath, and made a little puggy face at the door between them. Jo *was* capable, no doubt about it. She knew how to do a lot of things, but it was fun to find something she did not know how to do.

'Oh, I know,' came Jo's confident voice. 'Alec – my husband – his father worked for an antique dealer. He taught me a bit about it.'

'Thanks, Jo.' Dottie heard her own voice, a little too cool and distant, even allowing for the door between them, but was there *nothing* this woman could not do? 'I'll bear that in mind.'

When Keith looked round the other door to see what his aunt would like for supper, he was surprised to find Jo in a pair of denim overalls too big for her, sleeves rolled back and legs turned up over bare feet. She was paint-stained and work-manlike, but with that make-up, hair tied back in a jazzy scarf, and the tinkly bracelet, it was somehow like a stage costume, he thought.

'Is it that late?' Aunt Dorothy said. 'Are you hungry?'

'No, but I thought you must be.'

'I'll cook.' Aunt Dottie began to clean her brush. 'I'll make you my special fish pie. You're not eating enough these days.'

She tidied up her things neatly, and peeled off her rubber gloves, blowing into them like a nurse to pop the fingers out. Keith thought she might make a bigger pie and invite Jo to stay for supper, but she only said, 'Thanks so much, Jo, that's enough for the day. Come on, Fool.' She called to her dog, and went into the kitchen.

'I'll just finish this bit, then I'll go.' Jo was standing on a stool inside the door.

'They'll never get rid of the smell in here.' Keith sniffed what had been known as 'the smell in the library' ever since he could remember.

'It's the old books.'

'That's what they say, but have you looked in the locked cupboards? Could be a body.'

'Is that one of your fables?'

Keith enjoyed telling Jo, a new audience, some of The Sanctuary's myths and mysteries, time-worn, or invented to suit the occasion.

'Well, my grandmother Sylvia did die in here, you know.'

'Don't have me on.'

'Not this time, honest. As she got older, she sort of gradually began to shut up bits of the house until she ended up living in just the kitchen and this room, with a mattress on the floor and a smelly old dog. She wouldn't let anyone clean the place up, but Troutie kept on coming to do what she could. One morning, after she'd been away to Agnes's for a bank-holiday weekend, she found my grandmother with the dog in here – been dead for three days.'

'The dog too?'

'No.' Did Jo think he had made this up, to match Troutie and the budgerigar taking the last trip together? 'The dog was all right. It had eaten most of the food that Troutie had brought.' He wanted to add that it had begun to eat bits of Grandma Sylvia, but Jo would only believe so much.

Jo got down from the stool, and admired her door.

'It's beginning to look much better in here,' Keith said. 'I suppose Aunt Dottie must be trying to exorcise the ghost. Oh, sorry – you don't believe in that sort of thing, do you?'

'No, I don't.' Jo bent down to the paint pots on the floor, the ends of the gaudy scarf swinging over her shoulder.

'Pity, because if you did, I could tell you about the lilies.'

'What lilies?' Jo was kneeling down, cleaning brushes.

Keith's mother had once told him the story of the lilies, but Dorothy would never let it be talked about, or admit that it was true. He ought not to repeat it to Jo, but because he wanted to impress her, he was tempted to go on. 'Once when Uncle William came to see his mother, soon after he was married, Dorothy went upstairs and then she comes down and says to Sylvia, 'What's that overpowering smell in the big empty room at the corner?'

'"What smell?" Sylvia asks, sharp as a terrier.

'"Exotic, sort of churchy. Smells like dead lilies."

'"*Lilies*?" Sylvia is out of the room in a flash, and running half up the staircase. "Mother!" they hear her yell, in great fury. "What are you doing up there?"'

Keith put his hands in his pockets and looked at Jo solemnly. 'Now her mother,' he went on, 'had been dead for twenty-five years. She croaked in one of the first flu epidemics at the beginning of the war, in that corner room, where my uncle and aunt sleep now. She was laid out on her bed, with a great mass of hothouse lilies on her chest.'

It was disappointing that Jo only said, 'Oh, well,' rubbing paint cleaner into her hands, not impressed. 'You don't look very well, Keith,' she added.

'I'm fine.'

'I've heard that people with your illness can sometimes have relapses. Doesn't your mother worry, with you being here all summer, and not knowing how you are?'

'My mother,' Keith said flatly. 'Well, she'll be here soon. Then you'll see. She didn't want me to come here to recuperate, but Uncle William knew it was my best hope.'

'Do you still see your doctor?'

'I'm sick of doctors.'

'I don't blame you. You've had a rotten time.'

'Better days are coming.' Keith did feel stronger now, in a hopeful way that he had thought would never come to him again. 'If I stay away from the quacks, I know I'll be all right at Cambridge in October. Got to be. They're going to let me take a linguistics course.'

'Good for you. You certainly deserve it.'

Sometimes she came on a bit too hearty, spraying good cheer out of that exaggerated smile, but his ego was strong enough now to take nourishment, so he said, 'Thanks for the sympathy. People here – they do know about the illness, but being the kind of family they are, they still smell whiffs of hypochondria.'

'Like the lilies?' Jo laughed.

'Don't tell Aunt Dorothy I told you that story.'

'Of course not.'

'She swears now it never happened.'

'I can see why.'

Jo took a day off and went up to London to have her hair re-coloured and her eyebrows and lashes re-dyed.

'Still shooting the film?' Veronica asked. This was the reason Jo had given when she first walked into the hairdresser's in an unfamiliar part of London and asked to be made into a brunette.

'No, thank God. What a bore. But after all his complaints, my husband has decided he likes me this way, so I'll keep it for a bit.'

Having put about the story at The Sanctuary that she was tinting her hair because grey was coming in too early, Jo decided to reinforce that by having a few subtle streaks of silver-grey flecked into the front of the dark hair. She would answer comments with 'I can't fight the grey, so I'll exploit it, and prepare you all for seeing me snow white some day.' Thus she could go on touching up the roots of her fawn hair without arousing suspicion.

With the frosty streaks, she was more dramatic than ever. She and Veronica decided that it looked smashing, and since it was still early afternoon, Jo celebrated with a side trip to Acton on the way to the motorway.

In her disguise of dark glasses and headscarf and the old raincoat she kept in the back of the car, a reminder of the drab old Marigold who was rejected by William and Dorothy, Jo skulked about at the top of Brackett Road and was rewarded by the sight of Tessa and Rob coming out of the house. They headed down the hill, and turned left towards the park. It was thrilling to shadow someone who was unaware of being followed. When they paused at lights, or Rob stopped to fiddle with a sandal, or veer off to investigate something, like a dog, Jo turned away at once and studied a shop window, in case either of them looked round.

Good old Jo, turn her hand to anything, she can. Trail your husband, lady? Check on your wife? If she got fired as a tea-person, she could make a living as a private eye.

In the park, it was easy. She lay face down on the grass behind a tree, and watched Rob being a monkey in the adventure playground, while Tessa sat on a bench with the *au pair* girls and read a book.

After a while, Jo went back to Brackett Road to look into the uncurtained ground-floor room as she walked past. By the kerb near the house was a worn green car that looked somehow familiar. Of course. It was Chris Harvey's car. Jo had last seen it disgracing the weedless gravel in front of The Sanctuary, before Chris removed it modestly to the yard outside the garages. It sported a local residents' sticker inside the windscreen. Chris had moved in with Tessa.

Before she went to her own car a few streets away, Jo walked down to the post office, looked up the number of Tessa's firm, Maddox Management, and went into one of the phone booths.

'Could I speak to Theresa Taylor?'

'I'm sorry. She's not in the office this afternoon. Would you like to leave a message?'

'Yes, er – thank you. It's Mrs Christopher Harvey.' This was all said in a flat, Marigold voice, nothing like Jo's. 'Just tell her I rang.'

Tessa and Chris were going to Paris for three days.

'What *for*?' Rob kept asking.

'It's not *for* anything,' Tessa told him. 'Just for fun.'

'Then why aren't I going too?'

'Because Granny and Wum want you to stay with them.'

Tessa was trying not to do anything that might make Rob resent Chris. So far he liked him, and Chris was very good with Rob – calm and patient, helping him to draw and make plasticine models. When Chris went back to his Finchley flat to work in the pottery, Tessa sometimes took Rob up there. While she did some cleaning and tidying in the ground-floor flat, managing subtly to make it look less purely masculine, so that Chris would be aware of her when he was here alone, Rob messed about happily with wet clay alongside him in the garage, both of them humming.

Rob had even said, 'Must I go and see Dad before school starts?'

Tessa had said, mock-shocked, 'Of *course*. Poor Dad, he'd be terribly disappointed,' but secretly, her heart rose. She glanced at Chris, but he was carefully not looking or listening.

The three of them were happy in the house together. Tessa had not felt so hopeful about a man since she first cast herself blindly into the dazzle surrounding Rex. She felt quietly loved. She had gradually stopped seeing the half dozen useless men with whom she had been passing the time and trying to keep her ego nourished. Her work was going well. She had been given responsibility for two students in training. Christopher, who did not give away too much too quickly, was turning out to be the most worthwhile and warmly generous man on whom she had ever pinned her hopes. And they were going to have three days and nights on their own in Paris.

When they went down to The Sanctuary to leave Rob, most of the evening was spent making final plans for the Festival of the Lake. It was an ancient custom originated by Walter and Beatrice Cobb, mostly just for family and friends. Frederick and Geraldine had kept it going for a few years, because their son, the glorious Lionel, loved it (their daughter Sylvia hated it, like all parties). It was discontinued during the First War, and because Lionel died on the Somme in his twenty-first year, it was not started again until William decided to revive it a few years ago, not just for family and friends, but for anyone who wanted to come.

'Last year, we had nearly 800 people,' William told Christopher, 'and there may be more.'

There would be booths and tents for food and drink, and all the usual bakery and craft stalls and sideshows and games and competitions, the silver band in the nearly finished pavilion on low wooden supports over the marsh, jugglers, strolling musicians.

A firework firm had been hired, and a man who built boats in his back yard was transforming the two row boats into tiny gondolas, with prows and canopies outlined in fairy lights. Keith and a Cambridge friend would be in one, with guitars. Lee, the lovely woman who was known as 'Matthew's American', was bringing two friends, a tenor and a contralto, to sing old Neapolitan and Venetian love songs as the boats drifted up and down the lake, the oars flashing and glowing above and below the surface, if Rodney could get the underwater lamps fixed on to them.

They sat late on the terrace. When Tessa was first married to Rex, it had not been so peaceful here. Rex had been a good enough son-in-law, charming, amusing, showing off, arriving with bottles or smoked salmon or a new kitchen gadget from France or America, but when he was here, he made his own world, instead of adapting to theirs. He would fill the days with tennis, riding, golf, squash, phone calls, friends to be visited or to invite here, nights out in Oxford. He would not sit quietly and just talk for more than half an hour or so. That had suited Tessa then. She was infected with his restless energy. Now, with Christopher, she absorbed peacefulness, and felt closer to William and Dorothy.

The scent of the white nicotiana swelled and faded, like a pulse in the air. The stars were so bright that they were reflected in the lake, rocking in the ripples of something that plopped in the water.

Since the terrible episode of the doll being devoured by Flusher, Rob was more nervous of going upstairs than ever. He started the night on a sofa downstairs, and his mother would sleep in a room on the nursery floor.

'Shall I come up to you, or will you come down?' Christopher asked Tessa.

'I'll come down. He's fast asleep.'

Christopher was at the other end of the corridor from William and Dottie's room and the larger guest rooms. Tessa's girlhood bedroom was next to his, through an archway into the swell of the turret.

They stood by the window of Tessa's room and looked out at the amazing night, the bulldog statue as white as if there were a moon, and the massed heavy shapes of the trees across the park very dark against the starlit sky.

'You're quite sure you're not married?' Tessa had asked it six or seven times since she got the telephone message at the office.

'Surely I'd know.'

'But you'd be too kind to hurt me.'

'If I was kind and married, I wouldn't be here.'

'But, *Mrs Christopher Harvey*. Who on earth . . . ?'

'I told you. It's probably one of the women in my office, or in the store. There's a lot of jealousy and bitchiness in that place.'

'Perhaps they need another seminar: "How to resolve your emotional difficulties without making obscene phone calls."'

'Someone found out where you work, and decided to play games.'

'I'll kill them.'

'They can't hurt us,' he said peacefully. 'I don't know who it is, and I don't care.'

'Nor do I, my darling.'

In the park, on the other side of the wall where the shadow was deep, Jo continued to watch Tessa's window for quite a long time after the dimly seen figures moved back into the room, and the light went out.

Chapter Eleven

'You look tired.'

Dorothy saw Jo coming up to the pantry with baking tins at the end of the day.

'I'm never tired.' Jo always said that. 'I hope it's not my famous silver streaks. Do they make me look dreadfully old?'

Dottie never took bait. She said, 'Don't come in so early tomorrow. Have a lie in.'

'I've got to go to the shops. I'm out of things like sugar and coffee.'

'Rob and I are going shopping early. Tell me what you need and we'll drop it off on our way home.'

At Bramble Bank, Rob was fascinated by the small stream and the little bridge that led into Jo's front garden. The stream was quite meagre at this time of the year, and Rob stayed outside to plan a dam while his grandmother was in the house.

'You have made it nice, Jo.' The rooms were small but comfortable and not cluttered. 'I came here once or twice to see the Thompsons. They had a retarded child.'

'It had been done over before I came,' Jo said. 'I was lucky to find it.'

'What brought you here, after your husband died?'

'Oh ... old associations. Birdwatching. Walking on the Downs with Alec.' She looked away, as if her eyes were filling with tears.

'Is this him?' Dottie picked up the photograph of a young man with a small moustache, from a side table. Jo nodded without speaking. 'He looks like a lovely man. Poor Jo. He died of cancer, didn't he? Was he ill for a long time?' Dottie sat down, so that Jo could talk if she wanted to. She waited, drinking her coffee. 'Or don't you want to talk about it?'

Jo shook her head. She took the picture and looked at it for a long time before putting it back. Her face was quite different without the smile. It hung from her wide cheekbones, instead of rising up to them.

Outside, Mr Richardson saw Dorothy over the fence. 'Hullo, Dr Taylor.'

Dorothy remembered him. 'How nice to be able to see your beautiful vegetable garden. It used to be such a jungle here.'

'Done a lot of work, hasn't she? Josephine's a good neighbour.'

Rob had to be coaxed out of the stream, and did not want to get in the car with Dottie.

'You come again any time,' Jo told him.

'Can I, Granny?'

'If Jo doesn't mind.'

'I'd love it.'

'Soon, may I?'

'Of course.' Jo moved to kiss him, but didn't. Dorothy saw that she had discovered that if you bent to embrace Rob, he slithered away. Not rudely. He just suddenly wasn't there.

It was sooner than either Jo or Rob expected. The next day, Dottie's children's home in Witney had a crisis. They had organized the annual combined meeting of Special Homes in the region. Their big prize, the well-known child-abuse psychiatrist who was to be the opening speaker, was stranded by an airport strike in Greece. No one else was free in August at the last minute. Only Dr Taylor could do the job. Dorothy was a clear, down-to-earth speaker, with enough wit to keep an audience's attention, and enough knowledge and experience to tell them something new that they would not forget.

'I've got to do it.' She came into the tea-room soon after opening time when the only customers were a few who could not face the gardens without a stomach full of hot tea. 'Will is in London, and Rob was running a little temperature last night. I don't like to leave him with Keith. Ruth, could you possibly . . .?'

'Of course I could.' Ruth's warm downy cheeks lifted in a beam of pleasure. 'I always love to have him. Shall I take him home after work?'

'Oh, thanks, you're such a good friend, Ruth.'

'Hang on a minute, no, I'm not. Blow it, I forgot George's mother. It's her birthday. We've got to go over there, and she doesn't like small children. That's her own bad luck, but Rob would hate it. Oh, dear, I don't like to let you down.'

When Dorothy had gone out, Jo said to Ruth, 'I'd love to have Rob. Do you think she'd let me? He liked Bramble Bank, and she did say he could come and visit. Would they think I was pushy, if I –'

'You know they think the world of you, Jo, and I'd be ever so grateful, because then I wouldn't feel so bad. Go on, run after her – if you really want to have him. He can play you up, you know, to see what he can get away with.'

Now that it could pass as Ruth's idea, Jo made her offer to Dorothy, and was accepted.

'You'll understand that Rob is liable to be a bit insecure and demanding when his mother's away,' Dorothy explained. 'There's a continuing fear of abandonment, you see.'

'Because of his father?' Jo enjoyed asking.

'As with all children of broken homes.'

Yes, Doctor. As with wives.

Rob was delighted. 'You said I could come soon, but I didn't know it was as soon as this. You are quick for a grown-up, aren't you, Jo?'

He played in the stream outside with Charlotte, and came in for supper wet and sweltering and sat down at the table with filthy face and hands. It was a small round table that Jo had brought from London. In the pink corner house in Holland Park it had stood in the hall with its flaps down, and when she was Marigold Renshaw, she had imagined it going upstairs one day to be a nursery table. Now a child sat at this table at last. Jo gave Rob what he had asked for – Coca Cola and baked beans on toast – and did not tell him to go and wash his hands.

Rob hardly ate anything. He tried some ice-cream, then put his hot head in his hand and let tears fall from under his lank flop of front hair.

'Not hungry, Rob?' Jo sat opposite with a glass of wine, watching him.

'I want my Mum.'

Oh, of course. Marigold took over in a flash from kindly baby-sitter Jo, and dull rage poured through her like molten lead, weighing her down in mind and body. Somebody knocks themselves out for you, and because the ice-cream is the wrong flavour, it's, 'I want my Mum.'

'I daresay you do,' she said quite nastily, but not nastily enough to be reported back to Dorothy.

'When's my Mum coming to fetch me?'

Damn that bloody Tessa, a selfish doting mother of the worst kind, spoiling and worshipping but giving up nothing, and getting away with it. If she beat the child black and blue, he would still ask, 'Where's my Mum?'

'Soon.' Jo put her elbow on the table and her chin into her

hand, copying Rob's position. 'You don't look like her, do you?'

The golden image of Tessa sickened her. You could be mine, damn you, child – mine, the way I'm disguised now, with your dark hair and beautiful silky dark eyebrows that Rex gave you. If you were mine and Rex's, I would still possess him, through you.

'I don't know.' Rob whined and snuffled, trailing saliva strings through his tombstone teeth.

It was past his bedtime, but he would not go upstairs with Jo. He threw himself on the floor and picked at a gap in the worn fringe of the rug. Marigold had not brought her best things here, being only poor struggling widow Josephine. Rob pulled a cushion off the sofa and put his head on it and sucked his thumb. Dorothy was right about the insecurity. It would be easy for Jo–Marigold to play on that, but the child must like and trust her. That was vitally important. The whole family were Marigold's daggers against Tessa, but Rob was her ultimate weapon. In the end, she could do more harm by establishing his security with her.

Jo shook off the relentless weight of Marigold and said lightly, 'What does your mother do when you're a pest?' He did not answer. 'Does she whack you, or play a game with you?'

'What game?' Rob looked up.

'Snap, drawing – what would you like?'

They played a game of snap, and then Jo put him to bed and read to him until his straight spiky lashes fluttered and closed, and his face, pressed sideways into the pillow, performed the nightly childhood metamorphosis, as sudden and swift as death, into the original unsullied innocence of the world.

Jo's act when Dorothy was here had been good. If you can fool a psychologist, you can fool 'em all. Or, if you can't fool a psychologist, you can't fool anyone. Tears welling up . . . nice work, Jo. They were real, but not for non-existent Alec. There were plenty of genuine memories to summon them.

'How do you like being a birdwatcher?' she asked the photograph, putting it back on the shelf by its little cup of flowers.

When Dorothy had asked, 'What brought you here?' the man with the wild white hair who was always at The Sanctuary had popped into Jo's mind. Just before closing, he had come into the tea-room and had confided in Jo the real reason why he prowled about these grounds, and the passion of his life. That gave her the idea of adding birdwatching to her reasons for coming to this area.

Jo poured herself another large glass of wine. 'Have something to eat with it,' Alec suggested mildly from his frame on the shelf.

'Later. Don't interfere.'

Presently, she went up the short stairs to look at the sleeping child. Charlotte, curled up on the blanket, lifted her lip in an ugly little snarl. Rob's face was flushed, as if he had a touch of fever again. He had pushed down the bedclothes, and flung out his spindly arms. His narrow chest rose and fell rapidly, pushing out his rosy lips in rhythm. Above his collarless pyjama top, his frail neck throbbed like a bird's breast.

Charlotte jumped off the bed and followed Jo downstairs, looking suspicious. When Jo let her out into the garden, she barked outside the door. When she came in, she sat inside the front door, lifting her ears at imaginary sounds, lying down with her nose pointing under the door, jumping up when a car went by, to whine and bark.

'Shut up!' The dog was on the lookout for Tessa too.

Jo took off the false bosoms and the jewellery and the bright cyclamen cotton trousers she had worn for Dorothy, and pulled on a colourless shift, half-way between a smock and a night-dress, from the old days. She poured more wine with her back to Alec's picture, and wedged herself and her bare feet in the small rocking chair. She took off Alec's wedding ring and put it in her pocket. The mark of the broader, tighter ring which she had tugged off and thrown away after Rex left her was still visible under the knuckle. Holding that finger tightly with the other hand, she heard herself moan, and was overtaken by an avalanche of pain and loss.

If we'd had a child . . . if we'd had a child. The wine released the fruitless grieving that should have been used up long ago, but seemed to have an unending well-spring. If we'd had babies, I wouldn't have been able to work full time to support Rex while he made his way. 'He'll always be grateful to me . . .' I saw us in middle age, him telling people, 'Marigold made me what I am.' After Rex finally agreed to let Marigold stop the pill, month after month of disappointment followed. 'Just as well,' Rex had said. 'No time. We're free. I'm going places. Nothing can stop me. Why fret, Mari? Aren't I enough for you?'

Hunched in the chair, she could feel it now, from years ago, the vaguely full feeling, her breasts, those inadequate breasts, actually, visibly swelling, though still smaller than other women's. Not visible to Rex, and she wasn't going to tell him yet. She hugged the foetus to her, more precious as a secret. At about three months, she would go to the doctor, and then tell Rex.

At two and a half months, Rex told her that he was going to live with Tessa.

Oh, God, must I go through all the pain and agony again after all these years? You shouldn't have tanked yourself up with wine. Better get a whisky, Marigold, if you're going to crouch down here like a maggot, with that child upstairs – her child – Rex's child – and wallow.

With the whisky came a storm of weeping as she relived the ghastly scene with William and Dorothy in the rain, the nightmare drive back to London, the car crash, the ache of the seatbelt that did not ease when the pressure was released. Her agonizing sobs were almost like the convulsions that had racked her as she lay on the polished floor in the pink house, because she hadn't had the strength to climb on to the sofa. That night she had lived her own death, and when the tearing pains came and split her apart in a torrent of blood, she was living, or dying, through the death of her baby as well.

She did not tell Rex. He and Tessa never knew. Nobody knew. The few friends who were still in touch did not know why Marigold had been kept a whole week in the hospital after her so-called D and C. They did not know, because they did not see her, that she was not quite sane for half a year.

When it was the calendar time for her to give birth to Rex's baby, she took a tiny little boy from a pram outside a wool shop, and wandered vaguely off with him. No one knew. The grandmother ran after her. The baby was returned without fuss. The mother did not report it. The grandmother, red-faced, started up a bit of a commotion about, 'She might have killed him!', but the mother, who felt sorry for Marigold, shut her up.

Because she was grateful to the woman, Marigold saw the psychiatrist once again at the hospital where she had been taken after the miscarriage; but she did not tell him about the baby outside the wool shop, and he told her she was a strong, sensible woman who did not need him any more.

She had saved up enough of his pills to kill herself. But, because she was still not sane, she made the crazy mistake of ringing Rex to accuse Tessa of her death, after she took the pills, as she was passing out. Waking to the voice of the Welsh nurse scolding, 'You're a very silly girl, you might have died,' she was desperately disappointed and furious with herself and everyone else.

But if she had not made that wild mistake, Tessa would have gone free. Marigold would have lost the exquisite chance to become the avenging angel.

Very late in the night, about three o'clock, Jo went upstairs. When she turned out the light at the top of the stairs, she heard Rob cry out – a wail like a baby. He must be asleep. He cried out again, and then shouted loudly, as if he was sitting up, 'Mummy!'

'Mummy!' he cried again when Jo stood in the doorway. She turned on the light. He was standing up in bed, blinking and tottering.

'Lie down, Rob. It's not morning yet.'

'No!' He stepped off the bed and came to her, shivering, bony, and she took him to her room and into the bed with her.

He fell asleep again at once. Jo, who had survived the onslaught of Marigold tonight and was once more Jo, observed him sleeping. She tried to hate him, because of Tessa, but could not be bothered. Winning him over was easier, and more effective.

'You know what?' He woke her. He had been out early, humming tunelessly over his puny projects in the stream. 'I know how to make your bridge into a drawbridge. With a rope through the fork of that tree, we could lift it up from indoors.'

'Hooray.' Jo grabbed him for a quick hug, because he was alive and glowing and had all the pains of life ahead of him. 'You and I will live here in this castle and repel invaders.'

'For ever and ever?'

'Don't you want to go home?'

'I want to make a drawbridge.'

'Mummy will want you home,' Jo said. 'Mummy and Chris. Will Chris be at your home for ever and ever, do you think?'

Rob shrugged, bolting down cornflakes to get back outside. He could not give attention to anything beyond the present moment. So it was safe to say, 'You must miss being alone with Mummy now that Chris is always there.'

Rob was only half listening. He might not remember, but she dropped the thought into the pool of his consciousness, for luck.

Jo said later, 'Better go up and find your shoes and bring your bag down.'

'I'll come and stay with you again.'

'Have you had a good time?' Jo asked.

'Uh-huh.'

'So have I. I'm glad Chris made your mother leave you and go to Paris.'

Risky, but Charlotte was barking at the sound of a car in the lane, and Rob rushed out to scream at his grandmother, 'The drawbridge is up!'

Rob's visit was one more jewel in the crown of Jo the treasure. Her night of rage and remembered agony was a rare indulgence. She knew what her job was. Patiently and devotedly, she would continue to insinuate herself into the life of The Sanctuary.

Looking for the old porcelain pie-funnel for Jo to make her famous apple and bilberry pie as one of her contributions to the forthcoming Festival weekend, Dorothy opened cupboard doors below the long pantry counter.

'Look at all this stuff! I keep meaning to go through it, and there's never time. Incomplete early-morning tea-sets, soup cups with one handle missing, Geraldine's hot-chocolate set – look at the crack in this jug!'

'What a shame. It's eighteenth-century Derby, isn't it?'

Dorothy looked at Jo curiously. 'You know about china?'

'Well . . .' Jo had never talked about the museum job. She

was not supposed to be that class or quality of person. 'Alec's father taught me a bit. I loved that man. In the school holidays when I wasn't working' – it was all right for Jo to have been a teacher, like Marigold – 'I spent a lot of time with him at the antique shop.'

'You'll have to manage with an egg-cup instead of the pie-funnel,' Dottie said, 'unless it's in the dumb waiter.' She opened the small door in the wall above the old food-warming chests outside the pantry. 'Some of the stuff got put in here after the shaft was closed up.'

'Rob told me –' Jo began.

'I know.' Dorothy put some china oddments back in a shoe box and shut the dumb waiter door on them.

'Why is he afraid of it?'

'He and Annabel used to hide on the bottom shelf in there when they were smaller, until Dennis told Rob it would go down with him in it and never come up.'

'What are you going to do with those dear little Adderley flower baskets?' Jo asked, 'and the chocolate set?'

'Same as people before me did. Shut the door on them.'

'Perhaps I could –'

'Good God,' Dorothy said, smiling to cover her obvious irritation, 'is there nothing you can't do?'

'I'm sorry. Alec's father again.' Jo had acquired some ability to mend china at the museum. Like restoring books, it was one of what Rex used to call her 'useless skills'.

It was almost a month since poor old Mary Trout died in the fire. Although the family's distress had been considerable (which had gratified Jo) and they still talked about her often with nostalgia and regret, she had after all been a very old lady, ready to die, and the fatal fire was falling into place as one of the happenings of this summer.

Since Jo's merciful act of euthanasia, she had been making herself useful in other ways: being invaluable not only in the tea-room but increasingly in and around the house. It was time for another drama.

Dottie had snatched a couple of hours from the Festival preparations to finish the library doors with Jo. It was a cold, windy morning, but they had to have a window open.

Considerate Josephine noticed the gooseflesh on Dottie's bare arms, and said, 'I'll run up and get your sweatshirt for you. You're up a ladder and I'm not.'

Jo came back, looking puzzled. 'What's that strange smell?' She left open the door that led to the hall.

'Paint, what else?'

'No, it's on the first floor.'

Dottie came down from the step-ladder and went through to the foot of the stairs, then up the first flight. She came back. 'There's nothing. What sort of smell?'

'Like – it was sort of exotic. Like a very pungent, rotting flower scent.' Jo picked up her brush and turned away, fortunately. Dottie could not trust herself to go back up the ladder. Although she had put on her sweatshirt, she felt colder than before, and unusually shaky.

'I couldn't smell anything,' she told William when he came home, 'but the way Jo described it, it was like the – the scent of decaying lilies.'

William was not used to seeing his wife nervous, biting her lip, her cool blue eyes behind the rimless glasses troubled and uncertain. She had been watching for his car, and took him straight out to the terrace to talk.

'How could Jo have imagined that, Will?'

'You're sure she's never heard the story?'

'Ruth doesn't know about it. Nobody knows outside our

immediate family, and none of you have ever told anyone. Your sister Harriet did say something to Keith ages ago, as a sort of bad joke against your mother, but he says he didn't tell Jo. After I shut him up that night the Sterns were here – remember? – he got the message.'

'You trust him?' William thought Dottie was making rather heavy weather of this, but he took it seriously, because she was not a woman to be upset over nothing.

'A hundred per cent. Keith is very responsible now that he's well again.'

'Jo must have smelled something from the garden,' William said comfortably. 'Our bedroom windows are open.' He looked up. 'Don't worry, Dottie.'

Normally, you did not notice how small she was, because she carried herself so well, but when she was upset, she seemed smaller and less substantial. William put his arm round her and tried to make the right noises. They leaned on the balustrade above the dahlias and watched the long shadows of the last visitors moving slowly across the lawn towards the cypress walk.

'Anyway.' Dottie stood upright and was more solid again. 'I don't believe it ever really happened. I was only a silly young woman then, excited by being in love with you. I must have imagined smelling the dead lilies, or Sylvia did, because she was still psychologically tied to her mother.'

William wanted to agree, but she hated him to lie to her, so he said, 'It did happen. Ages ago. You were about twenty-five and not silly at all. You had on that white dress with a sort of sailor collar, like a child, and you'd gone up to see where we were going to sleep. I'll never forget you running down with your face quite white, and asking Sylvia, "What's that smell?" and my mother yelling up the stairs, "What are you doing up there, Mother!" and backing down again, shaking her fist and muttering, although Geraldine had been dead for more than twenty-five years. It gave me the creeps. I'll never forget it, and I know you haven't.'

'But I want to.' Dottie spoke through the haunting, dismissive notes of the Closing Bell. 'I want it not to have ever happened.'

Next day, Dorothy and William both left the house very early. Dorothy had arranged a lunch for some of the local people who were involved with the Festival, but she was late getting back from the clinic. The Dawsons, who were co-ordinating the food sales, the boat decorator and the man in charge of the fireworks display had already arrived. They had been given sherry and peanuts by Ruth, who was doing the lunch, so Dorothy took them into the dining-room as soon as she got home.

The Dawsons would have liked to linger, but Dorothy was in a hurry, so while they were finishing coffee, she went upstairs to get ready for her afternoon visits. The guests were in the front hall preparing to leave when Dorothy came downstairs.

'What's the matter, Dr Taylor?' The fireworks impresario took a step towards her. 'You don't look well.'

'Nothing's the matter.' Dorothy had a little difficulty focusing on him. Her voice sounded creaky to her, but no one must notice.

'It's this treacherous weather,' Mrs Dawson said, as Dorothy stepped down into the hall and picked up her bag and briefcase from a side table. 'Hot one day and cold the next. Does funny things to people.'

'Not to me.' Dorothy smiled and shook hands and thanked them for coming. She would not let herself look back upstairs. She did not need to breathe deeply to find out if the rotten, sickening smell had followed her. It was all through her, in her head and behind her eyes and in her mouth and nose, even her ears, and all the network of inner passages, like poison gas.

'You really don't look well.' The fireworks man still watched her.

'I'm fine. I'm preoccupied because I'm in a hurry, that's all. Please excuse me.'

'I don't know how I got through the afternoon, Will. I had two difficult children who were sulking, and one who has regressed, and a father who had stayed home from work to blame me for his son's brain damage. I was in a sort of daze, operating automatically. Poor people. I hope I wasn't short with them.

'I couldn't wait to get back here. I longed for it, and dreaded it. But when I got home and rushed upstairs, the smell – the smell of Geraldine's lilies – was . . . gone. Just a trace of it in the air. Can you smell it?'

William shook his head.

'You don't believe me.' Dorothy sat down on the big comfortable bed and looked miserably up at him. 'You know how Fool always follows me upstairs as if I were never going to come down again? When I went up after lunch, he didn't come. When I came down, he was sitting in the hall with those small ginger eyes peering anxiously through his face hair and one paw raised. Do you think dogs really are psychic?'

'I hope not. I'm sure this won't happen again.'

'It happened to Jo two days ago, and now to me. I can't say it's my imagination.'

'Dear Dottie.' William sat beside her and put their heads together. His hair was longer than hers. 'Let it go. It can't hurt us.'

'But it can!' Dorothy stood up and went to the window to look out, then turned to face him, very tense. 'That's the horrible thing. This house is safe and happy. Nothing goes wrong here. Nothing's ever gone wrong. But now – don't you feel it? It's somehow not quite the same any more.'

'It *is* the same,' William insisted, because he, too, had felt the faint chill stirrings of the wind of change, ever since Troutie's terrible death. 'You know it is, because we make it the same.'

'And I'm not prepared to give that up. That's why I never talked about the first time with the lilies and your mother, and why I wanted to push it down and bury it below my consciousness. That's why we mustn't tell anyone about this now. All's well, Will?' Dorothy put her neat head on one side.

'I suppose so.' William was in a state of confusion and unease. 'I've got to go outside for a while and think about this.'

'Nothing negative,' Dorothy ordered.

'That's not very realistic, for a professional.' William felt one side of his mouth lift up into the wry smile that Angela accused him of practising in the mirror.

'I'm not nearly as realistic as people think I am.' Dottie suddenly burst into tears and put her hands over her face.

Chapter Twelve

On Friday of the Festival weekend, everyone was very busy. Tents and booths were going up. Family and friends began to arrive, Rodney and Dennis and Keith and Tessa's Christopher were helping the electrician to wire up the coloured lights on the bridge and the terrace balustrade, and the floodlights on the trees.

Jo was helping Ruth, Mrs Smallbone, Brenda and Polly Dix in the house, and making endless tea, lemonade and sandwiches for the workers.

'Hullo!' enthused Tessa, following Rob, who had spotted Jo crossing the lawn with a tray and run full tilt at her. 'I do thank you for having Rob for the night.'

'I loved it.' The wide, candid Jo smile.

'So did he. You look good. I hear you've been working like a beaver and cooking non-stop. Aren't you worn out?'

'Never better.'

'You're a marvel.'

I am. I am the creator of psychic manifestations and phantasmagoria.

Jo felt that anything was within her reach. She had not felt so bold and powerful since – well, never in her whole life – not with her mother, who would not let her be a child; not with Rex the omnipotent; and certainly not after Rex.

Dorothy appeared to be her usual cool and efficient self. She gave no sign of distress, but Jo watched her. She watched everybody. Matthew brought Nina, his American friend Lee and her friends who were going to sing Italian love songs in the boat; William's sister Harriet came, opinionated and disposed to give orders to any willing helper like Jo; also a business friend of William's with his stunning wife who put every other woman in the shade.

William was so busy with last-minute details that he could hardly spend any time with Angela, but it was enough to know that she was there.

Their first meeting in London earlier in August had been for her to unload some of her feelings about her son. For their second meeting they had taken a picnic lunch to Regent's Park. William had brought the wine and Angela brought smoked-salmon sandwiches and watercress and peaches. They sat on the tired grass under a dark-green chestnut tree. The sky was the deeper blue that leads the summer towards autumn. The surrounding buildings stood at a distance, as if the park were immense. Traffic was only a background rumble.

'If anyone sees us,' William said, 'I don't care.'

'Because I don't count?' With her head lowered over the basket, Angela looked up at him under a spun-gold fall of hair.

'Because of how much you *do*,' William said recklessly, ignoring the inner clown who was making rude faces at him to stop.

They lay on the grass like young lovers.

When they walked back to their cars, Angela said, 'I think we won't meet any more.'

'But you know I invited Ralph to come to the Festival of the Lake, ages ago. Won't you –'

'I'll come, of course, Will. But don't embarrass me with that face.'

William said, 'Don't you embarrass *me*.'

'How?'

'By looking like you do.'

'I'll come in a cloak and chador,' Angela promised.

On Friday, William and Angela sat at one of the tables outside the tea-room and laughed a lot. Jo was interested. This must be the Lady Stern Ruth had talked about, whose son had been killed while she was staying at The Sanctuary at the end of May, before Jo came. What had been going on since then?

Jo brought out a jug of hot water and was introduced to the lady, who looked radiant.

As she turned away, Angela Stern dropped her voice, and Jo heard her say, 'Will – please. I told you in the park. Don't look at me with that face.'

'It's the only one I've got.' Boyish laugh.

Jo took a chance. Success had made her reckless. At home, she typed out a brief note:

> 'Dottie,
>
> I'm bringing this note down because I like you too much to say it to your face. I don't want to talk about it, but in case you've guessed that Will and I have been together, I want you to know it means nothing.
>
> A.'

When Jo came back later to help with dinner, she slipped upstairs while they were having coffee on the terrace, and put the note into the biography by Dorothy's side of the bed.

Perhaps she wouldn't read that book . . . Perhaps she'd go straight to sleep, or have a bit of a fumble with Wum, inflamed by the presence of the Lady Angela.

Worth a try.

The gardens were closed on Saturday afternoon. They were to

open at seven for the Festival. The dogs were fed early by Jo, very much in evidence in an Austrian-type dirndl dress with a bright cotton kerchief round her hair, making herself useful wherever she could.

'I'm feeding Charlotte,' Rob said. He was strung up and wildly excited. When you had waited so long for something, it was almost unbearable when it was actually on top of you. 'Open the tin for me, Jo.'

'Where is Charlotte?' she asked.

'I saw her a minute ago.'

The bigger dogs were snorting and gulping at their bowls. Rob ran round the kitchen and pantries and passages, calling, '*Charlotte!*' in the sing-song voice his mother used. Heading out of the china pantry and round the corner by the old warming chests, Rob heard a muffled yelp and a scrabbling. He screamed at the top of his voice and tugged open the door of the dumb waiter.

Charlotte was standing on the shelf, panting with a grin and wagging her tail; she didn't know what Rob knew, that in another moment she might have dropped out of sight into the basement kitchen where nobody ever went, and from where nobody would ever come back.

Rob snatched the little dog into his arms and faced Jo furiously.

'Only a joke.' She spread her hands and laughed. 'Charlotte likes playing hide-and-seek.'

'I'll tell my mother.' Rob scowled at her over the dog's woolly back.

'If you're going to be nasty,' Jo said, still laughing, 'I'll have to put *you* in the dumb waiter, won't I?'

Tessa, coming downstairs in her long peasant skirt and Mexican blouse – all the women of the house were to dress a bit exotically – met Rob stumping up with Charlotte in his arms.

'Has she had her dinner?'

'Yes.' He looked at the stair carpet.

'Has she really?'

'You and Chris never believe me.'

'Well, you don't always . . .' He did lie sometimes, especially when he was afraid, or excited, as he was now.

'Nobody believes me.'

'Put Charlotte down,' Tessa said patiently.

'She likes it.'

'She doesn't.' Charlotte's back legs were hanging uncomfortably and she was grumbling and resting her teeth against Rob's arm, which was the nearest she ever got to biting.

'You know what, Mum?'

'What?'

Rob dropped Charlotte, who shook herself and bounced downstairs.

'Do I know what, Rob?'

But he was jumping down after Charlotte, making sounds like a racing car. He often said, 'You know what?' when he had nothing to say, or 'Listen, Mum,' to get attention.

Tessa gave the dog her dinner and shut all the dogs up in the boot room, out of the way of the crowds.

William put on his blazer with The Sanctuary crest of sparring lambs, and went to lock the alpine house; he found that Jo had already remembered to do so. The gardens looked like a glorious carnival. People were coming in, and the Silver Band struck bravely up with 'March of the Gladiators'.

Ralph Stern was having a self-consciously jovial time, helping Jill and Annabel with the Italian ice-cream cart, but William could not see Angela anywhere.

'Told you I'd come in a chador, didn't I?'

At the touch on his arm, William turned to see an extravagantly shawled and beaded gypsy woman, thick black veil swathed round her head and face, heavy brown make-up, armfuls of bangles and huge gold hoop ear-rings that hung to her shoulders.

'My God, what –'

'Dottie's and my idea.'

Dottie stood by the opening of a small tent showily labelled 'Madame Shapiro and her Crystal Ball. She knows YOU better than YOU know YOURSELF!'

Angela draped the black veil over the lower part of her face and swished past her into the tent, fanning her exaggerated false eyelashes at William. 'Tell your fortune, Your Grace?'

'When you said a fortune teller, Dottie, I thought you meant a real one. You and she set this up?'

'To surprise you.'

Dottie was laughing at him, looking childish and more relaxed in a wide Chinese trouser-suit that swallowed her short neck and hid her small feet.

'Why didn't you tell me?' William felt clumsy and excluded.

Two young girls from the village approached, clutching each other, high heels sinking into the turf, and ducked into the lamplit tent in a frenzy of giggles.

'Peace, little missies,' Angela welcomed them in a deep throaty voice through a reek of joss sticks.

'It's fun.' Dottie moved William away. 'No one will know who she is. Even Ralph doesn't know. He's going round asking, "Where's my wife?" I'll make him go and have his fortune told.'

Clumsy and excluded or not, William was glad to see her so amused. 'You're feeling all right now, aren't you?' He looked in her face.

'Yes, Will.'

'Good girl.' William squeezed her arm through the silky

Chinese coat. 'Look at the crowds already. Listen to that lovely brassy music coming across the water. Hullo, John. Evening, Mrs Wright. Yes, isn't it? Oh, I'm glad you came, Warren. And your grandfather too – all the family – great. Look at those children, Dottie. Look at them running to the bridge as the coloured lights come on. How happy everybody is! This is going to be the best festival ever.'

As dusk fell, the tents and booths were lit up, and patches of the garden and the more spectacular trees and bushes were flooded with white light. Frank Pargeter arrived with Faye. He had wanted to come earlier and make his supper from the barbecues and ice-cream stalls, but Faye had got good liver out of the butcher today, so they had liver and bacon at home before they drove to The Sanctuary.

There was a huge crowd, hundreds of people. 'At five pounds a head,' Faye said, 'they're doing all right for themselves.'

'It's in aid of the RSPCA, you know that. Always been for animals, this place.' If Frank could have told the Taylors about 'his' nightingales, he might have got a donation for the Society for the Protection of Birds.

'I hope I shan't lose you in the crowd,' Faye grumbled. She often grumbled at the start of an outing, then had quite a good time. 'Better give me the keys of the car.'

'And let you drive off home without me?'

'Some of us have to get up early and go to work on Sundays.' Faye was doing overtime at the hospital, to pay for a conservatory.

Frank kept the keys, and they stayed together until Faye found friends and wandered off with them to try for prizes along the line of stalls, hoopla, roll-a-penny, coconut shies, bowling for the pig. Frank had two kinds of ice-cream, watched the jugglers and the Morris dancers, and joined the crowd singing along to old music hall tunes round the funny little bandstand at the shallow end of the lake. Where would the pintail ducks be hiding?

He met a friend in the beer tent and they went out together to look at the games and displays. At the bottle stall, they won a miniature of *crème de menthe* and a bottle of cough syrup. 'More or less the same thing,' said Frank. The cheery *Frau* in the Austrian dress behind the stall was the friendly woman from the tea-room who was such a good listener that Frank had run out of pretences about arboreal studies, and told her about birdwatching.

'How are the birds?' she asked.

'All right, I suppose,' Frank said vaguely. His friend was a birdwatcher too, and must not guess that he came to The Sanctuary often, and why.

Keith and Gregory, a friend from Cambridge, had spent most of the afternoon practising their guitar accompaniment with the singers Lee Foster had brought. Keith had not expected to enjoy anything else about the Festival, because he didn't like crowds of people hell-bent on mindless amusement; but when Lee asked him to show her around, he found himself getting excited, laughing immoderately at the jokes Lee made and at her American delight at so much Englishness erupting in one place under the cloudless night sky.

Because he was with her, and because he was keyed up about playing his guitar out on the lake, he felt hectic and feverish. He knew that syndrome. When you were low, you were prostrate, barely ticking over. When you were high everything was going at full tilt. He and Lee had a hot dog and drank ginger beer rather than alcohol because of Keith's illness. She was marvellous, quick and amused and perceptive, revelling in life. How could she put up with slow, old, quiet Matthew, who was at least fifteen years older? Keith was about fifteen years younger. Why didn't women look in that direction? They went with older men so they could always seem young, but if they would go with younger men, they would become young.

'*There* you are!' Matthew came out of the shadows with Nina. Lee spread her arms and put them round him with a delight that sent Keith's spirits plummeting.

On the floodlit lake, in the decorated boat behind the singers, he drooped over his guitar like a jilted lover, shivering in the warm evening, and trickled his stupid little soul out into the music. The love songs were sad enough for his mood. The woman's pure soaring voice and the man's sobbing tenor entreated each other to stay, to love for ever, to return to Sorrento, to remember, remember . . .

The voices carried clearly over the water as the illuminated boats drifted down the lake, the light-trimmed oars of the rowers flashing and dipping like phosphorescence. The noises of the crowd were stilled. Only a dog barked from time to time, far away in the house. Nina, who had been helping Jo and Ruth on the bakery stall, sat with Jo on the bank, absorbing the music through her hair, apparently enthralled by the emotional beauty of the scene. But when Jo said, 'Lee was clever to get hold of these lovely singers,' Nina pulled up a tuft of grass and said moodily, 'I was afraid she'd want to sing herself.'

'Is she good enough?'

'No,' Nina said with some bitterness, 'but she thinks she is.'

Jo, never one to miss an opportunity, asked softly, 'Did your mother come to The Sanctuary often?'

'Yes. She loved it.'

'You think about her a lot?'

'Of course.'

'It's been a rotten two years for you, hasn't it? It must be hard for you, Nina. It always is, when someone's been through so much with their father, and then he . . .' Between work on the stalls, Jo had been darting about among the crowds like a bandit working the Venetian back alleyways. She had been bought a beer by one of the gardeners and had knocked back a few glasses of wine, so she almost continued, 'And then he lets someone else come pushing in,' but she did not need to.

Nina was looking at her in hopeful surprise. 'Thanks,' she said. 'Everybody adores Lee – and she's OK, I suppose – but I'm glad someone seems to understand.'

When the singing was over, people began to gather on the house side of the lake to watch the fireworks. Many of them crowded on to the terrace in front of the house. Tessa and Chris were making their way up there with Rob, so that he could stand on the balustrade and clutch an urn, when Tessa saw her little dog running about anxiously among the strange legs, looking for her

'Charlotte!' Rob shrieked.

'I forgot about the cat flap. Here, *Char*-lotte! Here, little dog, here I am!'

At first Charlotte could not see where Tessa's voice came from. She darted back and forth, her ears flapping out sideways, panicking.

'*Char*-lotte!'

'Here she is!' Chris bent to grab her just as the first fireworks went up with a swoosh and a machine-gun clatter; the little dog dropped her tail and bolted down the terrace steps and off into the darkness.

'Sorry,' Chris said.

'She'll come back.'

'Of course, she always does.' Chris put an arm round Tessa

and she put an arm round Rob, tense and quivering on the balustrade, letting out screams shriller than any of the other children as each new coloured explosion of stars showered into the sky and fell in fizzling, diminishing flares into the lake.

The crowds left. Floodlights were turned off. Rodney and Dennis unplugged the strings of bulbs on the wooden bridge and went down to the lake to check that the boats were securely moored, then brought the batteries on shore.

Rob and Annabel had passed out and been carried to bed. Tessa and Chris, Nina, Keith and Gregory, William and Dorothy, Angela (Sir Ralph was on the phone to New York), Ruth and her husband, Jo, John and Polly Dix were all out with torches, searching to find Charlotte. The bigger dogs were running loose, but Charlotte had never had anything much to do with them. It was Tessa's call and whistle that would bring her out.

'*Char*-lotte! *Char*-lotte!'

'Let's give up for now, pet.' Chris was willing to search all night if that would help, but he knew that Tessa was exhausted. 'You know she'll come back by morning.'

'But supposing . . .' They had been over and over all that: caught by a branch through her collar, stuck in rabbit wire, broken a leg, trapped somehow.

'You'd hear her barking. She must have run a good way off, into fields or woods where she can't hear your voice. But she knows the way back.'

The others were returning to the house, telling Tessa those same things, which she knew, but only with her brain. The inner door to the boot room was left open, so that Charlotte, who was smaller than the largest black and white Tom, could come home the way she had got out, through the cat flap.

After everyone had gone to bed, Tessa, still in her Mexican

skirt, pulled a sweater over the low-necked blouse and went outside again and lay down under a rug on one of the long chairs on the terrace.

The perfect evening had chilled. The breeze off the lake was cold on her face as she stared out into the night beyond the wide terrace steps up which Charlotte would hop slowly, be-draggled and complaining, to find her. She dozed and woke and tried to stay awake. After dawn, with long shadows already travelling the wet grass, and the birds riotous, Tessa woke to a weight beside her feet.

'Charlotte!'

Her little boy was sitting on the rug, shivering in his pyjamas.

'Oh, darling Rob –'

His face dropped down and his mouth fell open in a square howl when he saw her begin to cry.

William, coming wearily downstairs to make tea, opened the dining-room curtains and saw the forlorn pair out there. He brought them in, made tea and put out cereal for Rob. Tessa took a mug up to wake Christopher, so that they could start searching again.

When William took the tray up to Dorothy, she sat up in her neat pyjamas and asked, 'Did the dog come back?'

William shook his head.

A short while later, someone knocked on the door. 'I hate to bother you.' It was Angela. 'But I've been so worried about the little dog. Any news?'

'Afraid not.'

'Oh, dear. I'll get dressed right away and start looking again.'

'I'll make you some breakfast first.' Dorothy got up and took clothes out of the walk-in cupboard.

William noticed that she went in and out of that cupboard rather quickly now. She had removed the big square mirror from the wall in there and hung it in the bedroom.

'Kind of Angela,' she said, dressing nimbly. 'She's really nice.'

'You and she are quite friendly, aren't you?' William said from the bathroom doorway.

'Good policy.' Dorothy gave a short, rather hard and un-Dottie-like laugh. 'If you can't beat 'em, join 'em. It's all right, Will. Don't look at me like a child caught stealing. I do know you've been seeing her in London.'

Only as a friend . . . to talk about her son . . . William discarded the whitewash and just said, 'How?'

'She told me.'

'*She* told you?' William came into the bedroom. 'Why?'

'I suppose she knew I wouldn't mind.'

'Don't you?'

'No.' Dottie gave him a smile that was tolerant, but patronizing. 'Does nobody any harm to have a little bit of a fling at this age.'

William was dressed in clean clothes, shaved, bathed, teeth cleaned, but he felt totally wrung out and dilapidated, as if it were the end of a devastating day. By knowing the very little there was to know about him and Angela, and not minding, Dorothy had mercilessly diffused the situation. The glamour and adventure were gone.

'"Young again and quite insane . . ."' Dottie went towards the door. 'Good for you to feel boyish, dear. It fits into your Peter Pan syndrome.'

They used to laugh about that, when Dottie was first studying psychology; she would come home with new clinical diagnoses and fit them on to William. But this was not a joke.

'That's not like you, Dottie.' She was never spiteful to him. 'What's got into you?'

He tried to stop her going out, but she said, 'Don't bother me. I'm so upset about poor Tessa's dog, I hardly know what I'm saying.'

Tessa was demented. She had to leave by midday to prepare for an early meeting in London tomorrow.

She rang up dozens of local people and went to the police station and drove about with Chris, putting up desperate little notices about Charlotte.

'Someone will find her. She's such a pretty dog, someone must have taken her in.'

Tessa could not react to, or even hear, the standard reassurances. Every time the phone rang, she snatched it up breathlessly, but it was always friends saying how wonderful the Festival had been.

'Thank God she's got that nice chap,' William said to Angela, after Chris had finally driven Tessa and Rob protectively away. 'He's the best she's had. But now, she'd rather have the dog.'

Angela had met William crossing the lawn, as he came back from saying a sad goodbye to Tessa at the garage.

'This is silly and I don't like to say it. I did bring the picture of my tortoiseshell cats for Bastet, but now –'

'Let's put it up.' William turned her towards the temple. 'There's always another animal. Life goes on. And for you and me, without each other, I suppose.' Angela said nothing. William added, 'Since Dottie knows.'

'Is that why she's been so nice to me?'

They went up the grass mound and into the small round temple.

'She said you'd told her.'

'Will – I didn't. Why on earth would I?'

'To make a fool of me?' William stood between two of the slender white pillars, looking out at the wreckage of the Festival on the lawns, while Angela was paying her respects to the aloof cat goddess on her pedestal, and sticking up her cat picture.

'She lied.'

'Dottie never lies.'

'She did this time. Look.' Angela stood close behind him. She gave off a kind of perfumed electricity that made him want to whip round and assault her. 'Whatever happens with us, it's all right, Will. It's all right.'

'It's not. She's spoiled it.' Sulky little boy. 'She – oh, I can't explain. She's – she's killed it.'

Chapter Thirteen

Charlotte never did come back. Tessa returned in a few days' time to wander desolately round the grounds, calling, whistling, but after that sad visit, she told William, 'I think I'll have to stay away for a while. If my little dog's not going to come back . . . I can't go on looking for ever; but I can't be here and not look for her. I'll be all right, Daddy, I swear I will. But for now, it's sort of – not the same.'

After Tessa had gone, he dwelt on her thought. It was not the same. Was it, for him, because he did not know if he would ever see Angela again? He was nearly fifty-six, on the downhill slope towards sixty. Could The Sanctuary no longer subscribe to the fiction of William as its little boy?

Dottie seemed more like herself again, as if the spiky little conversation in the bedroom had not happened, but William had an uneasy sense of slight, subtle changes creeping over his beloved home. Once, coming up from the drive on a dull day, he caught the house looking different. The corner turrets lowered at him a little. The creamy Cotswold stone seemed darker. Or was it only because there had been so much rain?

It was the end of summer, the closing in, the twilight approaching evening by evening. John Dix had told William that when the autumn work was done, he would be leaving to find work in the West Country. Did Polly really want to be near her mother when her baby was born, or had she and John sensed something wrong?

No one else seemed to notice anything. Visitors still wandered about the September gardens as peacefully as ever; but for William, the sense of content and security was slightly clouded, like the haze on an old mirror. Once or twice he thought he heard something in the night, and went down to check doors and windows. When he was alone in the great house, he had always loved the waiting spaces and the safe breathing silences. Now, at his desk, he might turn his head to the window, listening for Dottie, or swing round to look at the high solid door. Presently, he would get up and open the door. The flowers massed in the wide hall fireplace seemed excessive, like a wake. The clock ticked too loudly. What was this quality in the stillness? What was the house waiting for?

After the festival, Keith had been up most of the night searching for Charlotte. If he had not been so exhausted the next day, he might not have got into a fight with his mother, who had two large gin and tonics before lunch, and complained that Tessa had made more fuss about one disobedient mongrel than if she'd lost her child.

'Very clever.' Keith curled his lip across the table at her in the way he had learned at eleven. 'The minute she's gone, you manage to insult all three of them – Tessa, Charlotte, and Rob.'

'I'm only surprised' – Keith's mother reached for the bread basket – 'that there isn't more missing than just a dog. I've told you, Will, it's always been a mistake, letting every man and his uncle clutter up this place as if they owned it.'

Trying to divert trouble, Angela Stern had said sunnily, 'But Harriet, the visitors to the gardens, all those happy people who were here last night, surely none of them –'

'Any of them,' Sir Ralph interrupted her, 'given half a chance.'

'Without the visitors, we couldn't keep up the gardens,' William said patiently. He knew better than to say, 'I like them.'

'For your vanity.' Harriet could curl a lip too. She was drinking white wine on top of the gin. 'I saw you last night, lord of the manor: "Hullo there, Mr William. Evenin', mas'r Will."' Her Oxfordshire accent misfired. '"Done it again, you 'ave, ho ho, you Taylors."'

'Mother, shut *up*,' Keith growled. 'You're pissed.'

'Don't talk to me like that. You've been here too long. Give me some more of that potato salad.'

'I've had a great summer.' Keith did not pass her the bowl. She stretched across him.

'And you've worked for it,' his Uncle William told him.

'Work?' Harriet scoffed with her mouth full. 'He doesn't know the meaning of the word. You'd better pack up your things and come home with me this afternoon, Keith. You can put some stuff into the computer for your father until it's time to go to Cambridge.'

'You know I hate that.'

'You hate anything that means using your brain.'

After coffee and a nod over the Sunday papers, she said to Keith more reasonably, 'Ready in half an hour? I'll let you drive the new Audi if you want.'

'I've got a killer headache. I want only death.'

Jo, who had been helping Dorothy with lunch, heard him as she passed with a tray, and said in her eager, solicitous way, 'You look as if you might have a fever. Want me to take your temperature?'

'It's all right.' Keith had a thermometer in his room. He was used to monitoring his temperature during bad spells.

Jo came upstairs to him. 'I really do feel lousy,' he told her, flat on the bed.

'Same old thing?'

'I hope not. It's just, my mother gets me so wound up, and I'm worn out with looking for that wretched little dog, and seeing Tessa's face when she had to go. But I'm *better*, Jo. I'm not ill. I'm going to make it back to Cambridge. But I'm *not* going back with my mother today.'

'Want me to fix that for you?'

'Oh, yes. Dear, good Jo.' He groaned and turned his face into the pillow.

Dear, good Jo ran downstairs on a cushion of air. Ev-rything's go-ing my way! Keith is ill again, and I can outwit Harriet. Power corrupts, but Marigold is already corrupted.

Harriet was in the hall, nagging at Matthew, since she could not get far with William. She was the youngest, but she never gave up trying to straighten out her older brothers. 'I've told you, Matt. What you should do with Nina –'

'About Keith.' Jo beamed at her from the last few stairs.

'Where is he? I want to get going.'

'He's lying down. He wanted to get up, but honestly, I didn't think he should. Perhaps he should stay here. I'll help to look after him.'

'He's got into this neurotic pattern. If he can't get his own way, he says he's ill again.'

'He really is ill. A low fever, and some of the other symptoms recurring.'

'How do you know?'

Jo had read up on myalgic encephalomyelitis after she first met Keith. 'My brother-in-law had ME,' she invented. 'He'd get better and be all right for months, and then something would drag him down again.'

'Oh, blast,' said Keith's mother. 'I mean, I can say this to you because you seem to know him quite well. Are you sure he isn't faking?'

'I wish he was,' Jo said with simple tenderness.

By the middle of September, Keith was no better. His fever subsided, but he could not work, could hardly drag himself out of bed to study. Every morning, waking early at the bottom of a pit, he faced the dreadful doubt of whether it was worth making the effort to climb out.

'Do something, give me something,' he begged the London consultant. His college had agreed to let him take a second-year linguistics course, but if he could not start until January . . . 'I must get back to Cambridge next month.'

'You're not going anywhere,' the doctor said, 'except home. This new virus infection means complete mental and physical rest.'

His Aunt Dottie drove him back to The Sanctuary to pack up, then to his parents' house.

When she said, 'I'm so sorry,' Keith said, 'No, *I'm* sorry. Everything was going so well. But then – poor old Troutie incinerated, and Tessa losing Charlotte – I'm just one more thing that didn't go right this summer.'

Tessa kept her 'lost dog' notice in the local paper, and continued to check with the police and the animal shelter. She missed Charlotte all the time: when Rob tore downstairs alone to greet her coming home; at the chopping board in the kitchen where there was only emptiness waiting behind her; in the park, which had lost half its point without Charlotte running circles with Rob, coming down the slide on his lap, facing up to enormous dogs, dashing back constantly to make sure she knew where Tessa was.

Thank God she woke to find Chris in her bed. The weightless reminder that no one had sneaked up in the night to lie on

Tessa's far side was too painful to bear alone. Sometimes it could only be borne alone, and she wished Chris were not there, so that she could cry feeble hot tears into the pillow.

If she forgot for a while – working, talking to people, doing something she enjoyed – a sudden black sickening jolt would knock her off balance, dragging behind it the useless, agonizing images of Charlotte trapped, starving, terrified, dying betrayed and alone.

In some dreams, Charlotte was there and it had all been a dream within a dream. In others the little dog was tearing frantically about her with ears flapping, and Tessa could not get to her.

One day Rob said chattily, 'If Charlotte doesn't come back, we can get another dog.'

'Oh, Rob – don't.'

When they were alone, Chris said, 'You've got to admire a child's sensible attitude towards death.'

'You think I'm a sentimental idiot?'

'I want you happy again.'

'I *am*, with you. No one was ever so good to me.'

'Then come on, pet. Try to accept this rotten piece of bad luck. I'll find you another little dog who'll help you to get over it.'

'I adore you,' Tessa said mechanically, not because she wanted another dog – no dog, ever at all, except Charlotte – but to smother her resentment at his insensitivity.

When criticism surfaced in her – he was too passive, too content with an undemanding job, unambitious with his pottery – she pushed it back down in a panic. Christopher had never known the kind of wholesale demonstrative love that Tessa gave him, and she had never had the chance to give it to a man she could trust. Nothing must spoil that.

At the office, about two weeks after Charlotte was lost, Tessa picked up the phone on her desk.

'Theresa Taylor.'

Silence. Not a dead line. A sense of someone breathing, then the dial tone. An hour later, it happened again.

Tessa went out to lunch with Dr Ferullo and a woman in the Health department to discuss their workshop at the big autumn conference for hospital management.

'Any messages?' she asked when she came back.

'One call from a Mrs Christopher Harvey.'

Oh, God. 'Did she leave a number?'

'No, no message.'

Telling Chris, she said, 'Look, I don't *mind.* You must know that by now. Whoever there's been, if you've been married, are married, I don't care. But you've got to tell me.'

'Should I make something up to stop you agonizing? Listen, Tessa, I've told you everything about myself. You've got to believe me.'

'I *do.*' She stressed it tensely, because she must. Must believe. Mustn't let a pyschopath rattle her. Mustn't be robbed of what she had now.

The Sanctuary gardens were open to the public until the end of October. As the days shortened, the Closing Bell rang earlier each week to match the advancing dusk.

The visitors dwindled. A few of the specialist plantsmen came. The alpines, the chrysanthemum folk, the herbals, the hosta society. When half a dozen fern lovers came one Saturday, William got them to name and label the different varieties of which he had lost track.

Ruth had plugged in the hot-chocolate machine, but soon there were not enough visitors to make it worth keeping the tea-room open, even at weekends. After they closed it up for the winter, Jo still spent a lot of time at The Sanctuary. There were so many ways in which she could help, and wanted to help, that Dorothy put her on the regular domestic payroll.

Dorothy did not hand out fulsome praise. You earned anything you got, and if you knew you'd done a good job, that was your satisfaction. But once when Jo had helped Ruth with the tea-party for the children from the home, organizing games, changing babies, leading the donkey up and down long after everyone else had got sick of it, especially the donkey, Dorothy was moved to say, 'How did we ever get along without this woman?'

Jo and Marigold both purred. Indispensable. Marigold had never expected to be that to anyone.

Once, Rex had needed her. The children she taught at St Christopher's needed her. But as Rex made money and she left her job, the school survived without her, and Rex's need grew less and less until he could abandon her for an irresponsible egotist like Tessa.

Because Marigold had been nagged and jostled out of childhood – 'Grow up. Don't be a baby' – when she was pregnant, she knew that her own child was going to matter to her more than anything in the world. In bestowing a long enchanted childhood on this baby, Marigold would also be living in a world she had never known. When the baby was lost, her phantom childhood was lost for ever.

Now she was Jo, and Jo did matter. The Taylors needed her, set store by her, told friends, 'This is our remarkable Jo.'

Mrs Smallbone, born to grumble, never got used to Jo doing so much in the house. She would rather struggle to make a wide double bed alone than have Jo on the other side, halving the time and effort. When her rheumatism paid her out for this obstinacy, Jo was just there with an armful of sheets, taking the strain off her without triumph.

Clever old Jo. Marigold stood back and admired her for wooing Mrs Smallbone and for being careful, with Ruth, not to look like a usurper in the kitchen, because this house was *Ruth's*; it had been ever since she was a child helping her grandmother keep abreast of Miss Sylvia's casual neglect.

But in October, Ruth was busier in her own home. Her eldest son's girl-friend had been thrown out by her parents after she had her baby, and Ruth and George took her in. Torn between The Sanctuary and the needs of the baby and its hapless young mother, Ruth was one more person who said sincerely to Jo, 'What should I do without your help?'

With Jo's encouragement, Dorothy began to clear out some of the clutter of ages in the pantry cupboards. When she picked out a few items, like Geraldine's Derby chocolate jug, to be repaired, Jo set up a workshop in the library. She moved in an old work table and some bottles and jars and little mixing bowls.

'Now that I've got a good sticky mess going in there,' she said to William, 'why don't you let me work on some of the books for you as well?'

He laughed at her enthusiasm. 'Don't you ever stop?'

Not till I've done what I came here for.

One bleak grey afternoon, when there were only a few hardy couples walking in the garden among the russet leaves that fell faster than the gardeners could rake them up, Jo picked up *A Clerical History of the Western Parishes of the Vale of the White Horse* and brushed a small cloud of dust and spider legs out of it. She painted the damaged leather with Klucel and spirit, then put a piece of paper under the front cover and washed it.

While she was waiting for it to dry she wandered about the room, admiring the painting she had done, and comparing the front and back of the doors to see whether she or Dorothy had gilded the moulded wreaths more precisely. Running a critical eye over a wood panel in the space between the inner and outer doors, Jo saw that the paint with which Dorothy had sealed a vertical dry crack had flaked away for a few inches, as if one side of the wood had stirred fractionally and opened the crack again.

Why? Had the two panels ever not been completely joined? Was one of them a door? Jo eased a palette knife in carefully. More paint cracked away and the small panel opened a little on what seemed to be a shallow space. Not big enough for a cupboard, but – a hiding place?

Jo's imagination – or Marigold's – raced ahead to some amazing discovery, the reward for all her months of being Jo and working like a smiling slave. Something shocking, secret, scandalous. The tiny jewelled knife that killed the Reverend Hardcastle. The will – the missing will that would wreck lives. Sylvia's lost will that would prove William Taylor had no right to this great house.

By pulling very gently, she edged the panel forward enough to get her fingers inside. The tips touched crumbly wood immediately. It was just a dusty, very shallow empty space, about six inches square.

Jo drew out her fingers and pushed the wood shut carefully. It looked as it had looked before she investigated, like a crack between panels. No one would notice.

At the end of October, Frank Pargeter took his friend Roger to visit the Sanctuary gardens before they closed.

They had been out with a group to watch the water fowl on the lake at Blenheim Palace on a glorious early morning, with the sun breaking through the mist and peeling it away to reveal the splendours of the chimneys and finials and golden orbs that the great sleeping palace offered to the skies. Below, within a shallow bowl of frosted grass, the curving sweep of the lake teemed with life. They had seen tufted duck and great crested grebe and three gadwall asleep under the island dog-wood, and two of the new women who were learning to use their field guides excitedly identified a black-headed gull by a glimpse of its white forewing in flight.

Old hands like Frank and Roger preferred to watch birds alone, not in a group, but they liked to help new members, and it always gave Frank a thrill to see raw newcomers drawn in to the fascination of seeing and *naming*.

To see a bird was a delight. To name it was an unfettering kind of possession, a step closer between man and bird. Frank had observed that many visitors to The Sanctuary were captivated in this same way, by the *naming* of plants and flowers.

Moving his binoculars slowly along the farther shore, Frank caught a flash of brilliant green and blue.

'Last of the kingfishers.' He showed Roger, who reacted silently, with a smile that trembled a bit since his stroke, his small head in the badge-encrusted woollen cap nodding with slow appreciation.

It had been such a beautiful morning of friendship and shared pleasure that when they halted their slow wandering to lean on the parapet of the bridge and get out the Thermos, Frank found himself confiding in Roger his secret summer delight.

'Never see any of the little shy birds, do you, when you're in a group?' he began.

Roger shook his head peacefully.

'Never see any nightingales, would you, old son?'

Roger turned his head towards him.

'Got to be alone, like I've been.'

Roger raised his brindle furred eyebrows.

'Now that *my* precious pair have gone back to Africa, I'll take you to their breeding area, if you'll promise not to tell anyone.'

Roger's watery blue eyes were kind and steady. The corner of his mouth trembled. He knew and understood that after the traumas and dangers of the long migratory flights on which millions of small birds might be shot or trapped or limed by Mediterranean sportsmen, the nightingales must be protected if they came back to The Sanctuary.

'I trust you, old friend.' Frank put an arm round Roger's bony shoulder. 'I'll take you there.'

Faye had wanted Frank to go shopping with her in Oxford, but she had dropped one of the heavy brass hand-bells on her toes at Friday practice. So Frank drove Roger to The Sanctuary on Saturday, and paid both entrance fees, reduced for the end of the season.

'Nice to see you again before we close,' Mr Archer said. Although the gap in the wall had been Frank's favourite way of coming and going, he had paid to come in several times, to make it look all right, and to square his conscience.

Roger still walked with a stick and a trace of a limp, but he was fit again now, and quite nippy. His shorter strides kept up with Frank's lope up the deserted grass slope above the lake. Half-way up where the copse began on the left, Frank always stopped and turned round and raised his binoculars to scan the house and demesne, so that a suspicious watcher of his purposeful ascent might think he had gone for the view. Roger stopped too, and they admired a pair of mute swans, like floating salt cellars.

Then they moved over to the shelter of the trees, and were over the hill into the rough grass, picking their way through the undergrowth until they stood in the sacred spot where Frank had first seen the quick flitter of the nest-builders.

'Here's where I've lain and watched them. Here's where I've heard them sing.'

Roger was quite moved. Neither of them suggested searching for the remains of the nest. Even an invasion as distant as this might unnerve the nightingales if they came back next spring.

On their way to the cypress walk and the exit, Frank showed Roger some of the sights of the garden: the temple, the mausoleum, the oldest tree in Oxfordshire. Roger was particularly interested in the water-lilies which burgeoned profusely on the downstream side of the arched bridge. He had several species in his pond at home. It was getting late, but he stopped to poke about in the lake with his stick to find out at what depth the lilies were rooted.

Across the evening lawn came the first elegiac notes of the Closing Bell. *All . . . out . . .* it rang.

'Come on, old son.' Frank turned back half-way across the bridge.

All . . . out . . .

Roger had reversed his stick to fish for something. He was tugging at it with both hands. He shouted, and Frank went to help him. Together, they fished out a small sodden corpse, entangled in mud and weeds. A heavy carthorse shoe was tied to its neck with a piece of cord.

They laid it on the grass. Its eyes and mouth were full of black slimy mud. At first they could not see whether it was a dog or a large cat.

Frank crouched to pull away the water weeds. 'My God,' he said. It was the little dog that everyone had been running all over the countryside looking for after the Festival, the adored pet of William Taylor's daughter.

'Broken her poor heart, it has,' Josephine had told him later in the tea-room.

The Closing Bell had tolled into silence. Frank cut free the rusted horseshoe with his Swiss army knife and picked up the drowned dog.

Mr Archer had shut up the ticket hut and left. 'What shall we do?' Roger was distressed. Frank could not see any gardeners about, but there were lights in the ground floor of the house, so he carried the dog round to the front door and rang the bell. Roger stayed on the drive, poking miserably at the gravel with his stick.

William Taylor opened the door. He wore a sagging cardigan and held a pen in one hand and his glasses in the other. He looked at the dog and at Frank, dripping on the step, without comprehension for a moment.

'In the lake,' Frank said. 'Weight tied round its neck.'

Roger was carrying the horseshoe. He stepped forward and laid it on the bottom step. William Taylor took off his cardigan and wrapped the body of the dog in it. He looked about uncertainly for a moment and then stepped back into the hall.

Frank saw the small bundle in the cardigan dripping across the stone flags, before he shut the door and went down the steps to Roger.

Among the twenty or thirty visitors who came on Sunday to say goodbye to the Sanctuary gardens for the winter was Frank Pargeter. He found Tessa with her father and Chris watching Rob trying to paddle a canoe which was staked to the bank on a long rope.

'I felt I had to come.' The man took a stiff tweed hat off his white hair, which rose and began to blow randomly about at once.

'Thank you for –' Tessa made a helpless gesture towards the water. 'For finding my dog.' He remained there looking at them, his green corduroy trousers tucked into clumping footwear like ski boots. Did he want a tip or something?

'I wanted to come.' In his unhurried voice, the vowels were faintly Oxfordshire. 'To pay a last visit to your beautiful place. And I –' he looked at Tessa. 'I thought you might want to see where my friend found the little dog.'

'We know where the water-lilies are,' Tessa said shortly.

'And I thought – well, I was so sorry to be the bearer of bad news. I thought I ought to come back and bring you some that was good.'

His sympathetically serious face allowed itself a smile. Tessa looked at him blankly. He said to William, rather diffidently, 'You know I've been coming here a lot, and I'm afraid I told an untruth, because you see, I had a valuable secret.'

What on *earth?* Tessa frowned. Why do we have to have this?

'Yes?' William asked politely.

'It wasn't trees I was studying really. It was birds.'

'What's secret about that?'

'The birds I found, Mr Taylor. On the other side of the hill, a good way off in the rough part of the woods. I've been watching a pair of nightingales and their brood all summer.'

'Why keep it a secret?' Christopher asked.

'Because if they're disturbed, if the word gets about and people come crowding round, well – they scare easily. As it is,' he looked modestly down at the ski boots, 'I hope – I do believe that they might come back next spring.'

'That's great. Thanks.' William was pleased, but Tessa was angry. Bring good news! How dared he think his nightingales could even begin to make up in any way for Charlotte? She got up and went down the bank to pull on the rope and bring Rob in to shore.

'It's not time!'

'We're going indoors.'

'You *said*!' Feebly, Rob tried to push the paddle in the water against the pull of the rope. When the canoe nosed in to the bank, he dropped the paddle in the water and huddled down under the seat, wailing.

Frank Pargeter reached down a long arm and retrieved the paddle from the water before he put on the tweed hat and went tactfully away, throwing crumbs out of his pocket at a cruising pair of teal.

'Rob, come *out*.' Tessa put a foot in the light canoe, which rocked perilously. Chris pulled her back, grabbed the edge of the canoe to pull it alongside, and lifted the tense bundle of Rob out on to the grass.

'I hate you!' Rob attacked his legs with fists and teeth.

'Early bed,' William said automatically.

After Charlotte, or what was left of her, had been buried in the pet cemetery, the Frank Pargeter affair was being discussed in the kitchen, where Jo was making an early supper of sweet-and-sour pork and vegetable chow mein in the style that Keith had taught her. The family was increasingly free with what they talked about in front of Jo. When the Chinese meal was ready, she was going to stay and eat it with them.

'Who *is* this man?' Tessa wanted to know. 'I mean, who is he?'

Since the tragedy of Charlotte had been dragged up again, with her body, from the bottom of the lake, Tessa had fallen into a grumbling depression. 'He's been hanging about here all summer apparently. He was here on Festival night, because Christopher says he came twice to the hoopla stall, and won a jar of mustard. I think he's round the bend. How can we be sure he didn't drown my Charlotte out of some sick sort of spite and envy, or something. Although God knows, we don't seem to have much to envy.'

'How can we be sure there ever was a nightingale?' Chris asked William. 'He conveniently didn't tell you until they'd migrated.'

'But why would he lie?' William liked Frank, because he was fulsome about The Sanctuary.

'He admitted to me some time ago that he was a bird-watcher,' Jo said from the stove.

'You hear confessions in the tea-room?' Tessa said gloomily, hands round her drink on the table, not looking up.

'He told me a lot of stuff about ducks and thrushes and why pheasants are saved from extinction by being shot.' Jo turned round for her effect. *'But he never said a word about nightingales.'*

'Let it drop,' Dorothy said. 'Scapegoating won't bring Tessa's dog back. Anyway, suppose he did do it, for some bizarre reason, why would he fish her up two months later and bring her here?'

'A bluff?' Jo suggested. 'To make you say just what you've said.'

'There's no evidence against the man,' Dorothy said. 'There were hundreds of people there that night. Anyone could have done it.'

'But *why*?' Tessa went back and back to that. 'It's sick.'

'Want me to stop letting people come to The Sanctuary?' Her father stroked her hair, and she leaned against his shoulder.

'I don't know, Daddy. All I know is, someone's got a grudge against us, and that's horrible. Oh, hell. Everything is going wrong.'

Jo's cue to say brightly, as if she had not heard, 'It's just about ready, Tessa. Shall I go and call Rob?'

Rob was in the sitting-room watching something unsuitable on television.

'Better turn that off' – Jo did so – 'or Chris will be angry with you again.' She had not heard Chris scolding Rob, but he might have, since Rob had been acting up today. She might as well drop in a tickler.

The next day, coming from the downstairs cloakroom, Rob met Chris going there.

'Do up your zip,' Chris said.

'Always telling me!'

'Did you wash your hands?'

'Yes.' Chris was always going to nag, so Rob was always going to lie. Rob's mother was never angry with him. Why was Chris angry, like Jo said?

'Come here a sec, old man,' Chris said. 'I'll do up your shoelaces before you fall over them.'

'Not there.'

'Why?'

'You're standing by the dumb waiter and that's a bad place.'

'All right.' Chris moved to him. While he was on one knee tying the laces, Rob stuck out his lip and said to the top of his head, which was brown and soft like a dog, 'I miss Charlotte.'

'Of course you do. And I'm sure she misses you, wherever she is.' At least he didn't say 'in heaven' like some grown-ups.

'She isn't in the ground, you know. She got out. She's inside the dumb waiter.'

'Oh, stuff.' Chris sat back on his heels. 'You don't expect me to believe that?'

'She *is!*' Rob stamped both feet, one, two, like coming to attention at Cub marching. 'You know what?'

'What?' Chris smiled up at him, small teeth white through the beard, very doggy.

'Jo put her in there.'

'Come on, Rob.' Chris got up. 'Go and get the new spanner Wum gave you. We're going now.'

'She did, she did!' Whether Jo had done that before or after Charlotte drowned made no difference. Nobody believed Rob.

While they had been talking about Frank Pargeter, Jo had one of her genius ideas. Since he was under some family suspicion about the dog, and since this would be the last day he would come here until next spring, Jo made a detour through the gathering darkness on the way to her car, and, humming lightly, pushed the graceful statue of the proud cat-goddess Bastet off its pedestal in the temple. Let them suspect him of that too.

At Bramble Bank, Jo poured herself a large whisky. She never accepted anything except wine or sherry at The Sanctuary. With the second whisky, she sat down before Alec's picture.

Proud of me, aren't you, the way I pull things off? I have liquidated, so far, one useless old woman, a mute budgerigar and a spoiled lap dog. I've got everybody rattled, even old Dottie, who thought she was too rational and analytical to believe in the supernatural. A lot of them think that – you lot up there must laugh, those of you who are putting in the odd insubstantial appearance down here – until you actually confront them with a ghost.

But it's not enough. It's never enough. Vengeance is the gluttonous god. What next, Alec? Exterminate the furry lover? Still not enough. Tarty Miss Tessa would soon find another man. No. For our *pièce de résistance*, ladies and gentlemen . . .

Oh no, Josephine, you can't kill her. I must. *You're going too far.* Not far enough. Jo moved Alec's picture back and forth to indicate conversation. You don't think I can do it? *How?* Alec was always so literal. Wait and see. There's time.

Jo got up and stretched like a cat. 'I am the goddess Bastet, the all-powerful. I have plenty of time.'

Chapter Fourteen

Frank and Faye were both at home when William Taylor came to their house.

He sat on the edge of the chair by the electric fire and would not accept tea or coffee or anything to drink. Frank and Faye sat on the sofa and looked at him expectantly. Faye had on last winter's slippers, but she wasn't the kind of woman to mind that.

'Nice of you to let me come,' Mr Taylor said affably, but not at ease. 'I just wondered – well, I suppose you couldn't give us any clues about anyone at the Festival who might have drowned my daughter's dog? Did you see anything at all? It could have been done when the floodlights were turned out and everyone was watching the fireworks.'

'I'm sorry,' Frank said, 'I really am, Mr Taylor. I can't help you.'

'There's another mystery too.' William Taylor frowned and looked at his hands, folding and rubbing them. 'The – er, the statue of the cat in the little white temple. It was broken, probably some time on Sunday. I wondered if you happened to see anyone in there?'

Frank shook his head. 'I showed my friend the temple, but only from a distance, because it was late.'

'I see.' William cleared his throat. 'Well . . .' He stood up. 'I don't want to keep you if you're busy. I just thought . . .'

Embarrassed, he got himself out of the door and drove away.

'Faye.' Frank shut the front door and stood with his back against it. 'They think I did it. The dog, and now the cat statue. My God, they think it was me. Me who loves that place, who kept their nightingales safe, found their dog . . .'

'Ungrateful buggers.' Faye snapped her fingers in front of Frank's eyes, because he was staring into space. 'Don't look so shattered, Frank. Be angry. "Let the anger out," they're always telling old Mr Cassidy, and he comes scuttling down the hall like a crab and bangs his stick on my desk. I move my chair back. "Go it!" I say.'

'I can't.' Frank shook his head and went through to sit in the chair where William Taylor had sat. 'I'm just badly hurt, that's all.'

'Don't do them that favour,' Faye said. 'Don't let them hurt you. I know their sort.'

'No – no, you don't. They're good people. They love animals and flowers and all living things. That's what hurts. I like them.'

'Not now, you don't.' Faye folded her arms and looked down at him from her height.

'Yes, now. You think I'm daft – well, that's not news. Faye, I sort of – I love that family.'

'I know you do.' She smiled broadly, and he saw all the folds of her chins from below. 'I do think you're daft, but I understand.'

'No one else would.'

'Who cares? It's you and me, Frank. We know each other. We let each other be.'

When William went into the library to see how Jo was getting on with the books, he found her with a syringe, injecting wallpaper glue under a leather corner. Her glossy black hair swung forward into two crescents that nearly met across her face as she bent over the books.

'You are clever.' He watched her put a square of paper and cardboard over the corner and clamp it with a big clip.

'I found a book with drawings of the manor farm as it used to look before your ancestor rebuilt it into this noble pile.'

'There are stacks of papers put away somewhere,' William said, 'and the architect's drawings for the rebuilding. I always thought I might do something with them, if I ever retire. There's no proper history of this place, and there should be.'

'Why don't you get someone to start doing some of the research?' Jo put the glued book aside and examined the covers of another, fingering it lightly and with care.

'You want the job?' William liked to tease her about always volunteering for extra work.

'If you think I could do it.'

'I mean, I'd pay you, of course.'

'That isn't why I offered.'

'Don't get defensive.' William was not sure of Jo's financial situation. She owned her cottage, and her husband must have left her some money, or she would have found a full-time job, better paid than the tea-room. 'We could work something out.'

'I'd like that. Perhaps before you start looking out the papers, you could tell me some of the things you know about The Sanctuary's history, when you've got time.'

'Good idea. This room, for instance.' He looked at his watch, and sat down on the arm of one of the dark red leather chairs. 'When Desmond Cobb rebuilt the Elizabethan house in the eighteenth century, he had this room extended over some of the outbuildings, where the tea-room is now.'

'Was it always a library?'

'More or less. It was a billiard room too, before the last war, but when the Air Force was billeted here, they wrecked the table. It's had its ups and downs.'

'Your mother died in here, didn't she?' Jo looked up at him from under the symmetrically shaped brows and thick dark lashes.

'Yes, she did, actually.'

Troutie had telephoned him at the Bath office. 'On the lib'ry floor, Billie. She'd pulled down a whole lot of those boxes and piles of papers, as if she'd been trying to get up. Oh, I hate to tell you.'

'Where is she now?'

'Doctor Higgs and I got her on her bed. Bit of a job because Miss Sylvia was stiff, see, from laying there dead so long.'

'I'll be there as soon as I can. Who's with her?'

'Me, of course. And my Ruth's here.'

They were drinking soup out of cracked mugs in the cluttered clearing that was William's mother's living space at the kitchen end of the library, and beginning to shift the nearer outcrops of furniture and old newspapers and clothes and empty tin cans and dirty dog and cat dishes and rolled-up rugs which had accumulated round Sylvia all through the house as she moved from room to room in these last years.

They had laid her on the deplorable mattress which she had brought down here from the servants' corridor. Her thin face was contorted and bruised, as if she had fought her way out of life into death, her stiff grey hair sticking out on the hard yellowed pillow.

William had sunk down on the floor in a storm of weeping that took him completely by surprise.

His sister Harriet came with Matthew and they stayed in a hotel because there was no habitable bedroom in the house. 'No one ever quite gets over losing their mother, because they never get used to being nobody's child any more,' Harriet had said. 'It will be easier for us, though, since she was never really a proper mother.'

'That makes it worse!' William had cried, as loud as he could cry in the lounge of the Wheatsheaf, with three people watching television in the corner.

'How?'

He could not explain the black void – had never been able to describe to anyone, even Dottie, the vain relentless search for what you can never find.

Jo's November project was to get closer to William, and thus soften him up for the maximum pain.

Tessa's death was not worked out in detail. Jo was not yet ready to replace the luxury of bizarre, blood-curdling fantasies with a workmanlike plan. There were many tempting possibilities, easier to come by than your run-of-the-mill whodunnit murder, because Marigold, having achieved her ultimate revenge, would not really care whether she was caught or not. But however it was brought about, the mortification of having been conned into a trusting friendship with a black-haired woman with frosted streaks who did not exist would sharpen the agony of William's loss to the last excruciating edge.

The history of The Sanctuary was a lovely ploy. William loved to talk about this place. He told Jo things he remembered from his childhood, and things his grandparents and Mary Trout had told him from the past. Not things his mother had told him. They did not seem to have been close, and from what Jo had picked up in her magpie fashion, she had been a strange, solitary woman.

'She had a very hard life,' William told Jo, as they went through the churchyard gate to look at gravestones and memorial tablets. 'Her mother, Geraldine, was a strong-minded woman who always got her own way. She married Walter and Beatrice's eldest son, and they carried on the work of making a haven for animals and birds. Their only son was killed on the Somme.'

William showed Jo the ornate memorial plaque in the church:

> LIONEL WALTER COBB. 1895–1916.
> *O youths to come shall drink air warm and bright,*
> *Shall hear the bird cry in the sunny wood,*
> *All my Young England fell today in fight:*
> *That bird, that wood, was ransomed by our blood!*

'Sylvia was all they had left. It wasn't enough. She was about fourteen, shy, not pretty, bullied by her mother, who discouraged affection between her and her father. Troutie told me. She was sixteen then, a servant girl in her first job. Sit down a minute, and I'll tell you what else Troutie told me.'

They moved a couple of embroidered kneelers and sat in a front pew of the chilly little church.

'When Sylvia was about nineteen she fell passionately in love with a man called Jock, who was only alive because he'd been in railways during the war, instead of the Army. That made him "unsuitable", you see: the railways, and being alive. My mother couldn't marry him. He couldn't even come to the house – though he did secretly. He used to sneak in by the library window, over the roof of the harness room.'

William sat loosely on the narrow pew, hands between knees, looking rather wistfully at the bare altar and the small gilt eagle on the lectern. Jo watched his profile, listening with the right expression, if he should turn to her.

'Sylvia wasn't capable of defying her parents, but gradually, with the encouragement of Troutie, who was married herself by now, she began to plan how she would go off with Jock. But while she was still getting up her nerve to tell him, Jock got sick of being ostracized, and disappeared.'

'Oh, – poor Sylvia!' Jo cried, she hoped not too theatrically. 'What a tragedy.'

'It scarred her.' William closed his lips and thought for a moment. Then he turned to Jo with a brighter face. 'Ten years later, she married Eric Taylor, my father: older, unexciting, a solicitor for the land agents which later grew into my firm, Taylor and Birch.'

They went outside and he showed her his mother's grave: 'Wife of Eric and mother of William, Matthew and Harriet.' Nearby were Beatrice Cobb and Walter, removed from his first resting place in the mausoleum opposite Beatrice's bedroom window; the Reverend Hardcastle had been placed at a discreet distance.

'Are you going to put your mother's story into the history of The Sanctuary?' Jo asked.

'Not like that.' William laughed. His face was smiling and boyish again, after being serious in church. 'It's so sad, and for my mother's sake, it shouldn't be forgotten. So I told it to you because you're a good friend to this family, and you're interested.'

'I am all of that.' Jo bent to pull a thistle growing roughly above the navel of poor frustrated Sylvia, who seemed to have been one of the dimmer wits of this dynasty.

William went back to the garden, Jo to the village shop to get cough syrup and aspirin for Dorothy, who had gone off to work late with a sore throat, and might not get to the chemist. She was not quite so on top of things these days: less crisply efficient, occasionally forgetful.

The criminal who finally confesses to the cunningly sympathetic police-woman does himself a favour, as well as the police. He may regret the confession in the light of future events, but the unburdening itself felt good. Marigold was gaining from William's family stories, but he also liked telling them to understanding, concerned Jo.

Marigold had now been dear invaluable Jo, 'good friend to this family,' for almost six months, and occasionally, when Jo was most pleased with herself, Marigold butted in with irritated revulsion. *Stop being this sickening, Jo!* At first she had been able to snap out of it in an instant, and laugh at her performance and applaud it. Now she could not always do that. She would come home to Bramble Bank and not be able to stop being Jo, busy bee to the Taylors, by appointment. Ringing the house to remind Dorothy about Folly's steroid pill, sending a birthday card to Rob, dipping into the thick pile of papers and letters to make a show of extracting a few notes for William's history.

Remember me? Marigold could not always get back in. There had been times when she had decided: That's it. I can't stand this woman Jo any longer. I've got to abandon this charade and go away. But step by step, Jo led Marigold towards her goal: Flusher, Troutie, Geraldine's lilies, Charlotte, the statue of Bastet. It couldn't stop, until the end.

So Marigold had to let Jo go on, sucking up to William.

'Ever explored the cellars?' William asked. Jo shook her head. 'According to Troutie, a lot of the life of The Sanctuary happened down there, when she was a kitchen drudge.'

'Including the parlour-maid hanging herself in the game room?'

'Troutie found her. In her cap and apron – makes it worse, doesn't it? Come on, I'm going down to get some wine. I'll give you a quick tour.'

In the basement, he opened the doors of the stone-cold rooms, which had been the kitchen, scullery, game room, larders and servants' hall.

'When we were children, Matthew and I used to come down here to scare ourselves. These cellars had bad memories for Troutie. She told us to stay away, so of course we came. I saw a ghost here once.'

'I thought there were no ghosts at The Sanctuary.'

'No, honest. Right here in the kitchen. Through that high window the sun came swirling down in a wide beam of dust.' His eyes followed the memory down from the grimy half window under the vaulted brick ceiling. 'I saw something. Tall. White. Too tall. Thought I saw it, I suppose; it must have been the floating light, but I was petrified.' He could feel again the helpless terror, the shock that obliterated reason.

'What did you do?'

'Screamed and ran.'

'Who to?'

'My mother.'

Jo stood with her hands in the pockets of her plaid trousers, leaning against a stone shelf, waiting.

William turned round to her and said bitterly, 'I should have gone to Troutie.'

He took a step towards Jo, then stood back with his arms folded, and dropped his chin.

'Mother was busy. She was putting up camp beds. It was wartime, you know, and we were going to have evacuees. I was terrified – sick with terror. In fact, I *was* sick, on the floor. She stood and looked at it and then looked at me. She didn't know how to cope with it.'

'What did you do?'

'Cleaned up the sick, like she told me. No, Jo.' He lifted his head to see her reaction, afraid he had told too much. 'Don't misjudge. She couldn't cope. She could never cope with emotions, or people needing things from her. But it wasn't her fault. Her mother had shredded her confidence, kept her at home because she was the only one left, but always as a second best.'

Jo stood against the shelf, taking this in uncritically, but he said defensively, 'I suppose it wasn't Geraldine's fault either. She'd lost her beloved son. She was a tyrant, but she cherished this place. She tried to follow the ideals of Beatrice and Walter, and she needed Sylvia to help her.'

'She ruined her chance of love,' Jo said sadly.

'And do you know something? My mother never told me anything about that, ever. That's how badly she was crippled.'

'So she took it out on you.'

'No, it wasn't that.' William felt tormented. The loyal excuses came out with more difficulty, and were strangled by the truth. 'But she had nothing to give. Nothing, nothing, Jo, do you hear?' He was shouting, but nobody could hear through these dense underground walls. 'I never had a mother. I tried, I looked for every way to make her love me, but she had gone inside herself long ago, and there was no one there for me.'

Jo had come across the room to him, and when she put her arms round him, it felt natural, and so warm and protective that – oh, God, don't cry, you clown – 'I – sorry, Jo. I –'

'It's all right. Hush, it's all right. I know, I know . . .'

He did not take in what she said. It was just the murmuring and the safety, and he was the little boy Billie, with Troutie giving him what his mother never could, only Jo was supple and clean, not squashy and pungent like Troutie. But there was nothing sexual about the embrace of those strong arms, and the high firm breasts. It was so maternal that when she dropped her arms and he stepped back, it was not hastily, but slowly and naturally, and she said, 'All right now, Will?' and he said, 'Thanks.'

Help! What was happening? The avenging demon had turned

into a mother – and it was not an act. It wasn't Jo in that cobwebbed basement kitchen. It had been Marigold, reaching out to the child William with her empty arms. Save us. Jo was losing her grip. Better do something rotten quickly.

The Richardsons were away inspecting a new grandchild, and Jo was feeding their cats. In the bungalow, she automatically had a snoop round. Mrs Richardson's pillowcase of fabric scraps for her interminable cot quilt, which two grandchildren had already outgrown before it was finished, gave her an idea.

While the cats were feeding with voracious delicacy she picked through the multicoloured scraps and found a piece of rather coarse oatmeal linen, part of something like an old-fashioned child's smock.

She took it back to her cottage and cut it into a square, which she carefully hemmed with tiny stitches, as if it might be a man's handkerchief sewn by a woman long ago. In one corner, she embroidered the name 'Jock'. then she tore the handkerchief convincingly into three frayed pieces, so as not to look too perfect. Two of the pieces she put on her fire. The third, with part of the name on it, she dirtied up a bit and took to The Sanctuary.

'Have you got a moment?' Jo asked William when he came home and found her putting a steak and kidney pie together for weekend guests.

She took him to the end door of the library and stopped in the space between the outer and inner door.

'Did you know about this?' She put her hand on a painted wood panel.

'About what?'

She edged a blunt kitchen knife into a crack in the wood, and prised open a tiny door. 'It's like a little hiding hole.' She turned her bright-painted beam on him. 'I just discovered it.'

'Anything inside?'

'I didn't look.'

She was discreet. You had to give her that. William put his hand into the shallow space. Nothing there but a scrap of cloth. He brought it out and smoothed it. 'My God.' He showed it to Jo. 'My mother must have put this in there.'

'Is that the name of her – the man she loved?'

'Looks like it. Jock. She must have hidden it here after he'd gone, because this was the room where they met secretly.'

'That's romantic.' Jo looked at him mistily through those extravagant black eyelashes.

'Her favourite room.' William shut the little door and put the piece of cloth into his pocket. 'When she died here . . .' He had wanted to tell Jo this since he had confided in her in the underground kitchen. 'I found myself distraught. It didn't matter any more that she hadn't been the mother I wanted. For the first time, I was able to see her life from her point of view, and I was so desperately sorry for her.'

Curious. He had often talked to Dottie about Sylvia, whom she had diagnosed long ago as the 'not-good-enough mother', responsible for William's 'Peter Pan syndrome'; but he had never before talked to anyone outside the family, except Ruth, who knew a lot, since she had grown up with them.

Ruth had always been his good friend and confidante, but he did not see much of her these days. She had the baby at home, and its idiotic mother, of course, but – oh, Lord, he hadn't thought of this – might she feel that Jo was edging her out?

William went through the water meadows in search of her. The back door of Ruth's house was open, so he went in, as he always did. The draining-board was piled with dishes. Someone was playing loud music in the sitting-room. Ruth's husband George was sitting by the window with his bad leg up, reading the paper.

Ruth was sorting and folding a mountain of clothes in a laundry basket.

'Want some tea?'

She did not move towards the kettle, so he said, 'No, thanks,' and started to help her fold.

'Not like that.' She took the blue jeans from him. 'They're not pyjamas, Will.'

'I haven't seen you for ages,' he said. 'Everything all right?'

'Of course.' She raised her eyes to the ceiling, where the baby was crying in a particularly nasty way, and someone was clumping about. 'This place is like market day, that's all. I did give Dorothy a couple of mornings last week. Does she want me to come up at the weekend? Is that why you came?'

'I came to see you, silly. But if you could spare a bit of time, we've got three couples coming tomorrow, and I know Dottie would like some help in the kitchen.'

'Where's Jo then?'

'Well – she's already done some of the food, I think. She'll come back if she's needed, but I thought it would be nice to have you.'

'I'm very busy, Will.'

She had never said that before. Bringing up her children, helping with her grandmother, looking after George – she had never been too busy to come to The Sanctuary.

'Only because you want to do everything here yourself,' George put in from behind the paper. 'We can do a lot of this stuff. You go on up and give Dorothy a hand.'

'They don't need me *and* Jo.'

'Ruth.' William snatched baby garments away and held her hands. 'I want *you*.'

'Perhaps another time.' She picked up the baby clothes.

George said, 'Ruth,' mildly, but as if they'd talked about this before.

William said lamely, 'Well . . . come up soon. I want to show you something.'

'I might, if I get time.' She did not ask what he had to show her, so he did not tell her about the poignant discovery of the relic of Jock.

Ruth was changing. What was wrong? In the old days, if she had felt edged out by Jo, she would have said so.

Too much was changing. He still had the uncertain feeling that the house was in some ways subtly distancing itself. Instead of being part of them, it was watching them, waiting for something. How could he heal the unease? Filling it with people helped, and the weekend went well, although perhaps not quite as easily as usual. The guests left saying they had had a marvellous time, but William did not think they had; or was he putting himself in their places, allotting to them his own inexplicably dissatisfied feeling?

'What's wrong?' he asked Dottie, when they were alone.

'Don't always ask *me* what's wrong, Will. What's wrong with *you?*'

'I don't know. I just feel – everything feels, somehow, not quite right.'

'They all thought it was wonderful. They're coming back in a couple of weeks.'

'Oh, it was. It's just not . . . the same.'

'Still in love?' Dottie asked rather sharply.

'With you, of course.'

'Don't be childish. Are you still fretting for Angela Stern? Is that what's wrong?'

'Angela and I aren't going to see each other any more.'

'I don't mind either way. It doesn't matter.'

Clever Dottie. That attitude might have sent some men haring up to London. With William, it ensured that he would not.

William continued to be vaguely uneasy, and Dottie a little abrupt and scratchy. One evening she swore that she had smelled the death lilies again.

'It's your imagination.' William went up to the bedroom with her. 'You've got it on the brain.' He moved all over the room. 'There's not a trace.'

'Then I'm going mad.'

She slept in another room. In the morning she agreed that perhaps she had imagined it. A few days later, she made quite a bad mistake in the clinic, misdiagnosing the cause of a child's hyperactivity, and came home nervous, and upset with herself.

'You've been working too hard.' William tried to reassure her. 'You deserve a break.'

'I deserve nothing. I don't even deserve my job, if I make such a hash of it.'

About the middle of November, the lowering sun would strike through the pillars of the temple to flood the cat-goddess, who had symbolized to the Egyptians solar warmth and light.

This year, it struck the empty pedestal.

'Poor Bastet,' Dorothy said. 'I do miss her. I used to think she caught the last warmth of the sun, and held it until the next spring. Do you think I could ask Chris to make us another goddess?'

'Wouldn't be the same.'

Dorothy said quickly, 'You didn't like the hare he made?' putting criticism into William's mouth. 'You don't think he's any good.'

'He couldn't get the same elegance.'

'I don't see why.'

'Dottie.' William grabbed her arm. 'You're arguing for the sake of arguing.'

'What? Yes, so I am. How awful.'

She smiled, and he kissed the smile. 'Forget the cat.'

'I can't.'

'All right, in the New Year we'll take a trip. Get Christmas over, then we'll go to wherever you like – Florence, Siena. I'll find you another cat.'

'Shall we? It would be good to get away.'

Good to get away. That had never been a reason for going anywhere. Usually the best part of a trip abroad was coming home.

Dorothy and Jo were painting the library frieze, so that the room could be used at Christmas. When Tessa brought Rob for the weekend she found them both up on ladders.

'That looks like fun,' Tessa called up. 'Can I help?'

'Takes skill.' Her mother came down the ladder to embrace them both, while Jo, painting the plaster ferns and swags with an aching arm, fantasized what might happen to a ladder, so that Tessa would fall off and break her neck.

Tessa was going to Norwich with her boss. 'I'll try and get down on Sunday night,' she said. 'Otherwise, Rob will have to miss school, and I'll come as soon as I can on Monday. Have you got appointments, Mum? I'll have to get a train back to London to pick up the car.'

'Look, Tessa.' Jo was still at the top of her ladder. 'I'm going to London on Monday.' It was hair and eyebrow and eyelash time. 'I could bring Rob up to your house, and save you the drive. If you trust me.'

'Trust you? Heavens, you're a better driver than I am, and certainly better than Chris. He day-dreams. Would you really? I wouldn't want it to be a nuisance. Rob talks all the time in the car, when he's not being sick.'

'You can talk as much as you want,' Jo called down to Rob, 'and we'll stop at the service station and get choc ices.'

'Freez-O-Pops.' Rob stood at the bottom of the ladder, foreshortened to a dwarf needing a haircut. 'Can I climb up? Why not? You come down then, Jo. I want you to see the goats.'

Jo came down and pulled a sweater over her painting over-alls. Dorothy was showing Rob and Tessa the tiny secret cupboard between the doors. Rob would not put his hand in there. He backed away with his shoulders hunched. Tessa and her mother were mystified at his fear, so Jo felt pretty sure that he had not told anyone about Charlotte and the dumb waiter.

He did not seem to hold that against her. He went happily out with her to the small paddock, where they put out hay for the donkey and the goats, which was one of Jo's jobs on these winter afternoons. The pale cream billy goat with flecks of emerald in his eye did not pick up his own hay. He let the donkey take an overflowing jawful, and then pulled swags of it out of the donkey's mouth.

Rob was delirious. He had not seen the goat do that, so Jo said, 'I taught him,' and Rob shrieked with joy and clung round her waist and tried to pull her to the ground. She let him, and they rolled about in the cold wet grass, then jumped up to climb the gate and race to the house round the back paths and the walled garden, for cocoa and marshmallows.

William and Dorothy had people to dinner, so Rob stayed with Jo in the kitchen, until his grandmother took him up to bed in the room next to hers.

'I'm sorry, Jo.' She came down. 'He won't settle till you go up. Don't stay long. It's late.'

Jo could have stayed all night with the little boy. He was a very up-and-down child, but for some reason, he was being blissfully easy. Because his mother wasn't here? While Jo sang to him one of the funny repetitive songs from her teaching days, he lay wide-eyed, the sheet under his chin, mouth closed over the outsize teeth, soft and rosy.

Jo had always known that her baby would have been a boy, if the callous treachery of Tessa and Rex had not torn him bloodily from her too soon.

It was weeks since she had thought about her boy. Perhaps because William's anguish had revived her defeated maternal longings, she felt a powerful love for this skinny little boy in the bed who clutched her hand and said, 'Another! Another! Sing the fried-potato song.'

He did chatter all the way to London. He told feeble jokes from school, and they sang and played games. Jo was sorry when they turned into Brackett Road and found a parking space near the top of the hill. But going through the gate of number 47 and walking up the path and ringing the bell by the yellow door was breathtaking. At last Marigold was going inside the house where Tessa lived, was going to violate it with her presence and penetrate its charming secrets.

I love your house. Can I see the kitchen? Can I see upstairs?

Go ahead. Forgive the mess (it would be casually immaculate).

On the doorstep, Rob held Jo's hand and asked, 'Are you going to stay with us?'

'No, darling.'

'I want you to stay!' He looked up at her anxiously, but when the door opened, he dropped Jo's hand and rushed at Tessa and clung: 'Mummy Mummy where you been I missed you Mummy hullo my Mummy!'

'Thanks so much, Jo.' Crouching, Tessa smiled up over his agitated, butting head. Her hair was a fall of amber light. 'Come in and have some coffee.'

'No thanks.' Marigold could not go into the house. Although she had been longing to make its intimacies hers, she could hardly take in the details of the red-carpeted hall, the pictures and green plants, Chris's soft brown hat on a peg, the steep curve of the white stair rail.

Tessa's face, and her soft enfolding body and caressing hands incited Marigold to such a blinding agony of rage and envy that she could not move forward, could only say something about an appointment and back away, shut the door, stumble down the steps and out of the gate, away from the house where Tessa still had everything.

Gasping sobs without tears took away her breath as she struggled up the hill and fell into the safety of her car. If Tessa had looked out of the window, she would have seen that she did not drive away at once, and might have come out to see why, and found her with her arms on the wheel and her head down, fighting pain.

Gradually, her breathing slowed, her heart stopped pounding, the instrument of torture that clamped her head eased its grip. She drove away through the narrow streets where the parked cars of people like Tessa cared nothing for the passing cars of outsiders like Marigold.

Waiting at a red light, she was calm again, and in charge of herself. Her brain floated in a flat clear light of controlled intelligence. She knew now what she was going to do.

Death was not the purest revenge. Tessa must suffer, as Marigold had suffered. Nothing else would do.

It was not Tessa who must be killed. It was her child.

Chapter Fifteen

'What are you doing at Christmas?' Dorothy asked.

'I don't know. I might go to my sister,' Jo said without enthusiasm. 'And Alec's family have invited me.'

To be normal, she had to pretend she had friends or family to go to, which she didn't, looking like this. She had dropped everyone when she dropped the public Marigold, and nobody knew where she was.

Nobody cared, presumably. Marigold's family was only two aunts and a few cousins who had never been close. After Rex weeded out her teaching colleagues, who bored him, most of her friends had been people she had known with him and not wanted to see after he had murdered her life, even if they were on her side.

Presently, she invented a letter from Alec's mother, saying that they were all going to Canada after all, to spend Christmas with Frances and Don.

'Why don't you go?'

'Winnipeg? Too cold. And they haven't asked me. I'd rather stay here anyway.'

Dorothy was touched. 'You must have Christmas dinner with us.'

Keith, back at Cambridge, was much better. 'Another bloody clan gathering,' he groaned, but he was glad to be back at The

Sanctuary, and glad that the family was together at Christmas. They all were.

Make the most of it, Marigold gloated, while Jo was saying to everyone, 'How lovely to see you!' Marigold was going to ensure that none of them would ever enjoy Christmas again.

Harriet had brought her bull terrier, roughly the same shape as she was. Jill and Rodney had brought the spaniels. The house was full of dogs, getting underfoot, jostling for best place at the fire.

'I can still see my poor little Charlotte everywhere,' Tessa said dolefully to Jo. 'Bossing the other dogs, barking at the ducks, dashing into the kitchen every time someone lifts the lid of the biscuit jar.'

'You must miss her dreadfully.' Jo made the right kind of face. 'Will you ever get another?'

'I'd never find a dog like Charlotte. And the hurt's too great when they – if something happens.'

'Poor Tessa. I am sorry,' Jo said sincerely, while Marigold sniggered to herself over the bowl of turkey stuffing.

In the evening there were presents for everyone, including Jo. William and Dorothy had bought her a picture for her cottage. Rob gave her a lop-sided bowl he had made with Chris. Tessa gave her a charm for her bracelet.

'A little silver teapot. That's lovely.' Shows me where I belong.

After Christmas dinner and William's traditional toast of 'All's well', repeated by everyone with more or less conviction, Lee joined Keith at the piano.

'Time gone by . . . played a game . . .' they sang, then some of Keith's music, and other songs they both knew. Lee tried to make Matthew join her in a love song. His voice was terrible. He struggled, then laughed and retreated. 'You two get on with it.'

Softly and sweetly, they sang an old Christmas love song.

'They are wonderful together.' Jo tried that on Matthew to see if he minded. He agreed with amiable enthusiasm. To him, Keith was only a pale, skinny boy. He did not see that the boy was on fire.

They were still singing when Jo said she must go home, and went upstairs to the bathroom on the nursery floor.

Annabel was tucked up, neat, plump, still smug when asleep. The baby wallowed in an old-fashioned cot. Rob, with the blankets flung off the cabin bunk, breathed heavily through his mouth, flushed, his tousled hair damp. He often looked feverish when he was asleep.

Marigold covered him up. How was it done? The bedclothes pulled up and held down? The smothering pillow? A towel stuffed into the open mouth? It was almost too easy, with a child.

I'm sorry, Rob. To her amazement, tears welled up in Marigold's eyes and the great lashes blinked to catch them.

The drawing-room door had opened, and she could hear the piano. Feet were on the staircase. Jo left the room, opened and shut the door of the nursery bathroom, and started down the stairs.

Later that night, she came back to The Sanctuary.

Although the frieze was finished, they had not been able to use the library after all, because the radiators were tepid and the chimney had not been swept.

Keith took Lee into the library in the morning to show her Sylvia's secret cupboard. He was drawn to this grandmother who had died when he was little, the memory of her eccentric and romantically macabre.

They went in by the door from the dining-room. Lee stopped to look at the books. She was wearing slick American trousers and a massive soft sweater whose rolled collar flopped round the base of her long slender neck. She put on big owlish glasses and stood on the library step-ladder to read titles higher up. Her feet in soft red ballet slippers were small for her height and very narrow.

Leaning sideways, she lost her balance and reached out to Keith. Her hand on his shoulder sent a charge through him powerful enough to electrocute a fifteen-stone murderer. He pulled her down and lunged at her, grabbing handfuls of her and the voluminous sweater, mashing his face against hers, because she turned her mouth away.

'Listen.' He held her, breathing hard. 'I know I'm too young, and I'm sick and funny-looking . . .'

'Keith.' Lee looked at him with stern compassion. 'Your Uncle Matthew and I are going to be married.'

'I didn't know that.' He dropped his hands. He felt himself gaping.

She picked up her glasses. 'I thought everyone knew.'

'I've been so out of life, I guess its finer points have passed me by.'

'"Time gone by",' Lee quoted, with a smile. 'We'll still sing our songs though, huh?'

'Don't patronize me. The song ends,' he reminded her bitterly, '"Life? It's hollow."'

He was devastated. After she left the room, he fell into a leather chair with high sides. He thought he might be ill again. What would happen to him now?'

He stayed there until he was freezing cold. Then he went out by the door at the end of the room. Between the double doors, the secret panel had been torn open. It hung on one wrenched hinge, the wood splintered. Still shivering, Keith went to fetch his Uncle William.

*

It was not only the little cupboard. Looking round the library, William found between the sofa and the window a scattering of smashed china, recognizable as some of the pieces Jo had repaired and put on an alcove shelf.

'Call the police,' Harriet ordered.

'Nothing's stolen. No one's broken in.'

'Grill the children then.' Harriet was ready to do it herself. 'Who's been playing tricks?'

'A poltergeist,' Keith said glumly. The shock of the discovery had steadied him somewhat, and drained away feeling. With passion knocked out of him, he felt light-headed, as if he had taken pain-killers. 'Ask Nina.'

'Don't start on her.' Lee always defended Nina, although she was difficult, given to aggressive sulks, and often rude to her.

'What do you mean, a poltergeist?' Nina faced Keith angrily.

'It's the age, ducky. It happens to young girls. Things break. Pictures fly off walls. Watches stop.' He looked at his, and raised his eyebrows.

'I'll kill you!' Nina shouted.

Lee said, 'Lay off her, Keith,' and everybody was against him. But what did they want? Would they rather think that one of this stupid family had made this stupid mess deliberately?

When they had all gone, Jo could congratulate herself that she had indeed spoiled Christmas for them, although in a much less spectacular fashion than she had planned. The denouement could wait. There was time. Now that she knew she was capable of it, she could wait for exactly the right moment, and the delay had given her the chance to complete the little drama she had initiated when she put the torn scrap of Jock's nose-rag into what she had thus designated Sylvia's secret hiding place.

When she came back to The Sanctuary in the small hours after Christmas, she had left the car on the farm track off the road, walked up the drive carrying a rug, and climbed over the roof of the tea-room toilets, just as thrustful Jock used to do, and entered the library through the window she had unlatched before she went home earlier. Sounds of tearing wood and breaking china were muffled by the rug. The dogs were all at the other end of the house in various bedrooms. William's young outside labrador was in with his mother Corrie, because of a cut paw. Thus even dogs conspire to accommodate you if your heart is pure.

Next morning, although it was a holiday, Jo was in the kitchen in an apron quite early, having slipped into the library to fasten the window latch.

'Thanks for Christmas.' William said that to Dottie every year.

'Not one of our best. Who could possibly have done such a senseless thing? I can't believe any of the children . . . Nina is a bit upset about her father and Lee, but – oh, I don't want to think about it any more. Keith and that silly poltergeist stuff. I didn't like the look of him this morning.'

'Lucky it didn't occur to him,' William said heavily, 'that it might be my mother wreaking vengeance because I took her keepsake out of its hiding place.'

'Sylvia walks again?' Dottie thought he was joking, then realized. 'Oh no, for God's sake, Will, is that what you think?'

'Well, if Geraldine could come back . . . It was you smelled the lilies, Dottie, not me.'

'I don't believe it.'

'Nor do I, but what else would we prefer to believe?'

*

Two weeks in Italy settled them down, although they drove through storms and lashing rain, and did not find anything stylish enough to replace Bastet. They were both glad to get back to work, both hopeful that The Sanctuary and their life in it would recover the balance it had before things started to slip oddly sideways.

The house smelled warm and clean. Jo had brought flowering plants in from the greenhouse, and a little cushion of riotous pink Alpine splendour was on William's desk. His secretary had lined up letters and bills and magazines in neat, digestible piles on the dining-room table. Ruth had got in plenty of food.

Her son had got a caretaker's job and had moved out with his girl-friend and the baby. Ruth was regularly at the house, Jo was there less, and the two of them were spring-cleaning the tea-room in what seemed to be their old matey style.

The mild winter was anticipating spring with carpets of yellow aconite stars and dense drifts of snowdrops, the famous tall Sanctuary green-tips that Beatrice and Walter had first planted, brilliant white with clusters of green-edged petals within.

William spent contented hours with the new head gardener, familiarizing him with the gardens and planning the spring and summer campaign. He still spent time with Jo, to add to her notes for the history of The Sanctuary. She carried round a thick looseleaf binder, but was not ready to let him look at it yet.

She wanted to know more about the mausoleum, so William got the key to open the heavy doors, and took her inside. It was a dank and wretched place, a small cave inside the outer mound. On either side were thick stone tombs with slab lids, big enough to enclose coffins.

'What's in there?' Jo whispered, glancing back to the open

door to reassure herself that light and water and greenery were still outside.

'Nothing.' William slapped the vault where the Reverend Hardcastle had once rested. 'I told you. After Beatrice died, the bodies of her husband and her lover went with her to the churchyard.'

Jo read the carving over the door: '"Love is Eternal". . . It's thrilling,' she shivered. 'But I think I've had enough.'

It was Dottie's turn to put spring flowers into the church for Sunday service. That weekend, she and William were in London, so Jo had offered to arrange primroses and daffodils.

Coming out of the church as it was getting dark, on her way to return the keys to the vicarage, Jo saw two large young men with flat heads trying to prise an old headstone out of the ground with a crowbar.

'What are you doing?' she enquired mildly.

They stood their ground. One of them menaced her with the crowbar. 'Piss off,' he said.

'All right. I just wondered if you needed any help.'

'Piss off.'

She walked down the path, wanting to run, and gave them an inane grin as she passed, for self-protection. They had smashed the lock on the gate too. Before she reached it, she saw a chance to use this mindless force against the enemy. She turned. 'I just thought.' They were watching her. 'You fellows like old gravestones?'

'Yer.'

'Why?'

'Sell 'em.'

'Do you know about the tomb, over there at the big house, the one they call The Sanctuary?'

'What tomb?' one of them asked suspiciously.

'It's by the lake. There's some good old stone there, I heard, in a vault above ground.'

'So what?'

'So nothing.' She was still a chirpy, harmless lady, a bit barmy. 'I found it interesting, and I thought you might too.'

'Heard the latest, Faye?'

Frank came home from the shops and found his wife in from her afternoon's digging in the cold lumpy soil, lying on the floor because of her back.

'You're the one who gets out to hear all the news,' she said in the gruff, blunt voice that meant she was in a good mood.

'Those poor Taylors. They've had enough this year, I should have thought. Now it's the mausoleum.'

'Someone buried alive?'

'Somebody broke in there last night when they were away. Smashed in those thick doors with an iron bar or something, and prised the lids off the tombs.'

'Body snatchers,' Faye said sagely, on her back, chin tucked in, big breasts flopped out sideways.

'No bodies in there, so the vandals left a few messages in spray paint.'

'And I suppose the Taylors will think you did that too,' Faye said throatily, because her bronchial tubes were at the wrong angle.

'I thought I'd slip up there next week when the gardens open and let you know how much damage has been done.'

'Not to mention having a look to see what the birds and waterfowl are up to.'

'Does that annoy you?'

'I'm glad you have a hobby. Keeps you off the street.'

'You're good to me.' He smiled down at her.

'It's because I'm on my back. You're easier to take from this angle.'

As it was opening day, Frank paid to go in to The Sanctuary. He crossed the marsh boardwalk and went straight through the copse and over to the other side of the hill. Most of the trees and bushes were bare, but the undergrowth where the birds had nested was still an impenetrable tangle. He would have to wait until there was a chance of seeing one of them in flight before he would know whether they had come back again this year. In a month, three weeks perhaps, in this early spring . . . soon, soon he would know.

Down by the lake the mausoleum was roped off, with a warning notice. One of the doors had been forced open outwards. It hung crookedly, the metal smashed and buckled, as if by an angry giant. The violence of the damage was a brutal, incongruous scar on the peace and beauty of the gardens.

The Taylors' grandson was running about with a chubby friend, scrapping and tumbling each other, rolling in combat down the sloping lawn.

'Steady on,' Frank said as he passed near them to take a closer look at the mausoleum.

The fatter boy stared. The boy called Rob scrambled up and said bossily, 'If you go near the mouse-o-leum, they'll get you.'

'Who will?'

'The dead people. The skeleton of Hardcastle. He broke down the door and came bursting out. I knew he would.'

'I'm not afraid.' Frank liked this funny little boy who flung himself so eagerly into fear or excitement.

Rob screamed and ran off shouting, the slower boy tagging along behind.

Coming from the cypress walk after exchanging spring greetings with Mr Archer in the ticket hut, Jo saw Rob talking to the birdwatcher.

When he screamed and plunged away, she wanted to run after him, chase him through the shrubbery, and finish him off like a hare.

The fat boy panted up to her. 'Which way did he go?'

'That way.' Jo pointed in the wrong direction, but Rob pranced out of the bushes and yelled, 'Silly bugger – wait till I get you!'

Yes, Rob, wait. My poor little Rob. Soon now. Soon.

It was to be sooner than she thought.

In the village where Jo lived she had been pleasant to everybody, so as not to arouse comment, but she had not made friends, beyond knowing a few people to speak to in the shop.

When she went in for bread, Priscilla Smythe was there, with a round-shouldered man in a hat like a tweed basin whose back was turned.

'*Hul*-lo, Jo.' Priscilla was always gracious to second-class citizens like widows. 'Larry, this is Jo Kennedy who lives in one of those enchanting little cottages by the stream.'

Larry turned round from the shelves with a mean moon face, and Jo wanted to run. Those rolled disgruntled lips, the little seeking eyes. It was Lawrence Pratt, who used to come to the pink house in Holland Park, before he tried to make trouble for Rex over a dodgy project, and was jettisoned.

'Morning.' Lawrence nodded without interest, then his eyes sharpened and he frowned under the silly hat. 'I know you, don't I?'

'I don't think so.' Jo stretched her smile to be even more Jo and less Marigold, and kept her voice high and theatrical. 'Excuse me, I've got to run.'

Damn Lawrence. Jo walked away fast, without her bread.

Could he really suspect dim, colourless Marigold behind the make-up and the flashy manner and the black hair with the dramatic frosted streaks? Oh, God – to have everything blown apart now by a cunning fool like Lawrence Pratt!

Out of sight of the shop, she began to run. She scurried across her bridge and through the cottage door like a field animal, then sat down with her coat on to slow her agitated heart and get her breath.

Steady, Josephine. Alec called her that when he was taking charge.

I'm afraid.

Don't panic. Alec never panicked or wavered. *Lawrence couldn't have recognized you in that moment. He's not psychic.*

But Lawrence Pratt came with his stooped walk along the lane past Bramble Bank, and stopped to look quite intrusively over the bridge and the gate, straight at the downstairs window where Jo stood back out of sight, and wished him dead.

Rob was to go to his father at Easter. His grandmother would drive him to High Wycombe on Good Friday.

Dorothy was tired. Patients, meetings, reports to write, and hours of free clinic time for the agency in London had been building up to an uncharacteristic tension and weariness.

'Let me do this . . . let me do that for you,' Jo would urge.

'Don't indulge me. I'll fall apart.'

The tea-room was to open at the weekend, with Ruth's hot-cross buns and Jo's simnel cake. Although she was still agitated and full of an indecisive fear that was more Marigold than Jo, she stayed up late on Thursday to bake the simnel cakes. Jo was like that, even in a crisis. Thoughtful for the pleasure of others.

As a reward, the inspiration came to her, in a flash of pure clear light as she was washing cake tins at the sink. Doubt fled. Anxiety was gone. This was it, then.

Go to bed, Alec suggested, as she paced about in a state of charged excitement. She took his picture outside and flung it far over the back hedge into the darkness of the impenetrable brambles.

On Friday morning, Jo went up to the house early with the cakes and offered to drive Rob to High Wycombe. Dorothy was not even up and dressed. She talked to Jo out of her bedroom window.

'You're a treasure,' she said. 'I won't forget this, Jo.'

No, Dottie, I don't think you will.

Jo went to the bank and drew out all the money from the Josephine Kennedy account that she had obtained by giving her real name of Marigold Renshaw as a reference. Then she went back to Bramble Bank for her bags, and took from the top of the wardrobe her father's old service revolver, the Webley Scott 45 that she had found at the house after her mother died. She put the two bags in the boot of the car and locked it, so that Dorothy could not open it to put Rob's stuff in there.

'Can I climb through to the front seat now that Granny can't see?' Rob was delighted to be driving with Jo, because she drove faster than his grandmother.

'No, Rob. It's against the law.'

'You don't care about that.'

'I have to.' To be stopped by the police for having a small child in the front seat would be one of those ironically stupid mistakes that foiled the most inspired schemes of people in books.

'This isn't the road we take to go to Dad's.'

'We're going a new way. This will be more fun, you'll see.'

Jo was heading west. Short of sleep and light-headed, she imagined Wales, perhaps, or up to Birmingham, and on to Scotland. Could you go to the Isle of Man without a passport? Dorothy had said that Rob was not expected at any particular time. How long would it be safe to stay on the road in this car? How long before a nation-wide search of hotels and bed-and-breakfasts began? It was one thing to disappear by herself and have her hair bleached out and be Marigold again; quite another to disappear with a child for whom everyone was looking.

Infirm of purpose! She was fully awake. This morning's sloppy, euphoric idea that she could somehow kidnap Rob and vanish would not stand up against what she knew in her heart was the only possible ending to the saga of her revenge. *Give me the daggers.*

She stopped to buy something to eat and drink, and she and Rob sat with it in the back seat, and she told him a story about a boy and his travels. Stories either put Rob over the top with excitement, or made him sleepy. He leaned against her, his dark tousled hair against her breast.

She propped him against the window and quickly took off the padded bra with its hard twin cones that were the hallmark of Jo's shirts and sweaters, then drew him to her again and put her arms round him and sat for a long time, hidden from the road on the track into a wood, his head against the smaller, softer breast of Marigold.

Do it here? Here? Now? She would lead him deep into the wood and lie him down and put the gun to his head while he was sleeping, then throw it far into the trees and walk back to the car alone.

To what? Her hard and ruthless campaign was against Tessa and her family, not against Rob. Could the real Marigold really snuff out his life and walk away?

No wonder she had never looked realistically beyond the deed when she was brewing her plans. There was no beyond for her, that was the truth of it. If killing Rob was her final revenge on Tessa, then the last act of her life's drama was done, and her own death the final curtain.

She left Rob, and with shaking hands, took from her bag the sleeping pills she had brought in case he was excitable and difficult.

'Wake up for a minute, Rob.'

'No.' He pushed her away and snuggled into the corner of the back seat.

'Here. I've got a pill for you. Mummy says you're to take it like a good boy. Look, there's some Coke left.'

When he was half awake, she fumbled the pill into his mouth and tipped in the remains of the Coca-Cola. He coughed and spluttered, but the pill stayed down. He cried a little when she laid him down on the seat, but was soon asleep again.

Jo drove on slowly, because her mind was a turmoil of thoughts and panicky visions. She saw herself finding a disused garage, driving in, and with the door shut and the engine running, holding Rob down by the exhaust, then lying down herself to breathe in its deadly fumes. They said it paralysed you very quickly, so that even if you tried to move away, you couldn't.

She saw a car crash at a hundred miles an hour, the bodies unrecognizable within the concertina of distorted metal. Trees near the road, telegraph poles, the abutment of a bridge – was this the one? Was this?

Too late, she had gone past, too slowly. On a straight road she speeded up and watched each car that came towards her. It would be so simple to turn the wheel and swerve across the road into a head-on collision. Why didn't she do it?

Because this wasn't it. In a crackling explosion of light, like fireworks over the lake, she understood. The door into the mausoleum was open. With her own mischievous words in the churchyard, she had set the stage for the ultimate assault: her final inspired legacy to all the Taylors.

'Love is Eternal' Beatrice had declared in stone. For ever

and ever, eternally, William and Dorothy and their descendants would see the mausoleum from the windows of the house, and they would never forget.

Jo turned the car and drove back fast towards The Sanctuary.

At this time of year, the Sanctuary gardens were closed at twilight, the bell in the tall cypress ringing a little later each day as the evenings lightened.

Avoiding the village, Jo drove by a back road to the side of the estate near the church. Would there be a service on Good Friday evening? The church was dark, the small car park empty. She drove down the narrow lane to where gardeners and grave-diggers left their trucks, and stopped her car out of sight behind a hedge.

With the loaded gun in the pocket of her jacket, she carried Rob into the churchyard. He did not weigh much, poor skinny baby, although he was heavily asleep. She laid him down behind the wall and waited with him until the visitors would have left the gardens.

She wanted dusk, and dreaded it. Give me a little more time. Don't let it be dusk! But although she stretched her eyes to prolong the day, inexorably the light faded, and in the distance, she heard the tolling of the Closing Bell.

Up in the copse, sitting on a dead tree with his feet on a crumbling mat of dry bracken, Frank heard the bell and abandoned his fruitless watch. After this weekend, he would use his old route over the broken wall, but at Easter, and especially on Good Friday, it had not seemed right to cheat.

He extricated himself from the undergrowth and tangled grass, and dropped easily down the slope in his heavy boots. Looking all about him in the gathering twilight, to enjoy the leafing out of the tall trees and the blossom and the patches of bright colour still holding the light, Frank saw a figure move out from the shadows of the laurels that lined the pathway to the church. The figure was carrying something quite large and moving with a sideways gait along the upper bank of the lake. As he got nearer he saw that it was a woman, carrying a child.

Someone hurt? Frank hurried down to see if he could help.

Rob's sleeping body grew heavier and heavier. To get under the double rope barrier, Jo had to put him down, crawl through and pull him after her.

He woke, without opening his eyes, on the marble step of the tomb, and wailed, feebly.

'It's all right, darling. Jo's here. Come on.' Her arms were too tired to pick him up again, so she half carried him, dragging his feet, through the smashed door.

Inside the tomb Jo could dimly see that the stone slabs had been replaced on the vaults. She lifted Rob and laid him gently down on one of them. She would put the gun to his head, then lie down on the other side at once, a triumphant Juliet, and shoot herself.

Asleep again, the child lay quite peacefully on his side on the cold stone. After she had brought out the gun, Jo laid it down and took off her jacket. She bundled it up and put it carefully under Rob's head.

A shout. A scrabble and thudding of feet down from the top of the mound. Jo picked up the gun and held it behind her back as a man with a torch pushed through the gap between the doors.

'What's wrong?' His breath was quick and harsh. 'What are you doing?'

'Get out!'

'No, the child shouldn't be in there. Get his death of cold. Here – wake up, Rob!' he said loudly.

He pulled the limp boy outside. Jo followed and he turned back, holding Rob, his torch full on her face.

What he saw there made him grab at her. She raised the gun and shot wildly at Rob, then turned the gun against herself.

Up at the house, they were lighting a fire and drawing curtains. Dorothy was clearing away the tea things. Tessa, who had come with Chris, was thinking that she would soon ring Rex's house to say goodnight to Rob.

They all heard a double shot.

By the lake they found Jo dead, her shattered head hanging half into the water. Frank was dead, or dying. Rob was on the overgrown steps above the mausoleum, moaning feebly, his arms flung out over the stone mastiff that crouched there: 'Faithful unto Death.'

Chapter Sixteen

After a long time, life at The Sanctuary settled down and grew peaceful again. The gardens were closed for a year, and when they reopened the following spring the mausoleum had been torn down and the mound flattened and grassed over, so that there was nothing to be peered at by ghoulish sightseers.

There was a noticeable increase in visitors, and occasionally still another journalist. No questions were answered by the gardeners, or Ruth in the tea-room. They had learned to say, 'I didn't work here last year.'

'I wish that were true, Will,' Ruth said, more than once. 'I torture myself thinking there must have been some way I could have known.'

Papers at Bramble Bank had told them who Jo was. Publicity had brought an aunt and cousin, a few friends, a man who had been staying with Priscilla Smythe. Most of the mysteries had been gradually cleared up, except for the great central mystery of how they could all have been so totally deceived by Marigold's performance as Jo.

'We wanted to be, I suppose,' Ruth said. 'She was so blooming useful. Right from the beginning, when she turned up to help me in the tea-room, she seemed like just what we needed.'

'And there *are* women like that. Over-made-up and theatrical, cheerful, pushy. I rather liked her,' Tessa said sadly.

'I liked her very much.' William thought about the strange

scene in the underground kitchen, where Jo, as he realized now, was being Marigold, and giving him her real self.

They had all liked her. Jill did say, 'I always found her a bit over-powering,' but it was only Harriet who boasted, 'I knew all along there was something bogus about her,' and nobody believed that.

One evening in June, William and Frank Pargeter's friend Roger, who had looked for the nightingales last year in vain, made a twilight pilgrimage to the thicket at the top of the hill. There was some general bird movement and warbler song, and what seemed like nesting activity. They waited quietly. Roger never said much anyway.

After a while, they heard it, over-riding the other birds. The loud clear, clicking call, and then the bubbling trill.

The nightingales had come back again.

Roger muttered, looking at William with his crooked smile, 'Frank's epitaph. He saved the birds.'

'He also saved my grandson.'

Frank had lived for two days after the operation on the stomach wound. Whispering, his wife interpreting, he had managed to tell them what had happened at the tomb.

Now the family did not talk about that any more, nor about the things that had happened while Jo was at The Sanctuary. After Frank died, clutching Faye's hand, they had talked and talked endlessly, reasoning, remembering, until everything had been explained.

Troutie's death. Poor Charlotte. Perhaps the hare in the hidden garden. Probably Bastet. The keepsake of Sylvia's lover and the destruction in the library.

When the rooms where John and Polly Dix had once lived were being looked at for conversion into a separate flat, they remembered that there was a crawl space under the central roof to the attics of the other turret wing. On the floor, where a trapdoor had been cut in the boards, Dorothy found transparent, long-dead lily petals and a few curled dry leaves.

The shock of discovering that Jo was responsible for psychic phenomena had been quickly overtaken by relief that they had not been genuine mysteries.

'And perhaps I never did smell those lilies in the first place,' Dorothy said.

'You did. And my mother did shout up the stairs.'

'She could have imagined that Geraldine had come back to haunt her. Anyway, nothing like that can ever happen again. I remember telling Ralph Stern two years ago, "No supernatural phenomena here," rather pompously, but he was so full of himself. The Sanctuary is safe, Will.'

'All's well.'

The nightmare was over. The house was theirs again. The garden entranced itself in luminous bloom and beauty, and shed its untroubled peace once more on the gentle visitors who came to wander and enjoy.

They held the Festival of the Lake again, because life goes on, and tradition heals its own wounds. Tessa and Rob and Chris did not come, but when the summer was almost over, they had a last family weekend, before the children went back to school.

In the kitchen before dinner, Jill and Tessa were feeding children and cooking, and William was making drinks in the butler's pantry.

He put a glass on the table for Dottie, who was playing cards with Rob and Annabel.

'What's the matter, Wum?' Rob's eyes followed William's towards the door of the back pantry where cakes were prepared for the tea-room. The door had been closed. It was opening very slowly. Then it stopped, not far enough to see into the pantry. They would normally have looked away and started to talk again, because not all the doors shut properly or hung level in this old house.

But they were all still, staring in silence. The sound was quite faint, but clear, like the light jingle of a woman's bracelets as she moved her arm.